Playing
Sarah Bernhardt

a novel

Joan Givner

SIMON & PIERRE FICTION
A MEMBER OF THE DUNDURN GROUP
TORONTO

Editor: Barry Jowett
Copy-editor: Jennifer Bergeron
Design: Jennifer Scott
Printer: Webcom

Library and Archives Canada Cataloguing in Publication

Givner, Joan, 1936–
    Playing Sarah Bernhardt / Joan Givner.

ISBN 1-55002-537-6

1. De la Roche, Mazo, 1879–1961 — Fiction. I. Title.

PS8563.I86P53 2004   C813'.54   C2004-903710-2

1   2   3   4   5   08   07   06   05   04

We acknowledge the support of the **Canada Council for the Arts** and the **Ontario Arts Council** for our publishing program. We also acknowledge the financial support of the **Government of Canada** through the **Book Publishing Industry Development Program** and **The Association for the Export of Canadian Books**, and the **Government of Ontario** through the **Ontario Book Publishers Tax Credit** program.

Care has been taken to trace the ownership of copyright material used in this book. The author and the publisher welcome any information enabling them to rectify any references or credit in subsequent editions.

J. Kirk Howard, President

Printed and bound in Canada.
Printed on recycled paper.
www.dundurn.com

Dundurn Press
8 Market Street, Suite 200
Toronto, Ontario, Canada
M5E 1M6

Gazelle Book Services Limited
White Cross Mills
Hightown, Lancaster, England
LA1 4X5

Dundurn Press
2250 Military Road
Tonawanda NY
U.S.A. 14150

Author's Note

Biographical information about the relationship of Mazo de la Roche and Caroline Clement is based on my book *Mazo de la Roche: The Hidden Life* (Toronto: Oxford University Press, 1989). The dramatic scenes are adapted from my play *Mazo and Caroline*, which was performed at the Saskatchewan Playwrights Centre's Spring Festival in 1992. The part of the novel dealing with the origin (about which nothing is known) and life of Mazo's adopted child is pure fiction. Any resemblance to actual people is coincidental.

I

She was playing Sarah Bernhardt when it happened. Perhaps that was part of it, for Sarah herself had been plagued by stage fright. "Le trac," she called it, "fear." There were two kinds, Sarah said, "the kind that sends you mad, and the kind that paralyzes." The whole cast would wait in horror while Sarah stood transfixed, speechless. Of course, it might have been a trick to create suspense. That would have been in character, too, because she always staged a dramatic recovery.

Harriet hadn't recovered. Not on the first night, not on the second, not on the third. Each time she was striding across the stage when she was suddenly struck dumb, every part of her body frozen — her limbs, her vocal chords, her mind. It happened always at the mid-point in the play. So there was no alternative but to quit.

The voices rose around her in a chorus, like the women of Thebes, scolding and predicting doom.

"You can't run away from it."

"Just lay off the sauce, Harriet, and you'll be OK."

"See somebody. Get professional help and give it another try."

"You can't just run away."

Oh, yes, you can. She ran away, speeding down the long, straight highway and into the foothills of the Rockies. She drove recklessly, taking the hairpin bends too fast and choosing the most dangerous roads. She stopped for gas and bought stale sandwiches and weak coffee in paper cups and picked up a newspaper, though newspapers never interested her. The theatre was her timeless world and its gossip her daily news. But she stopped in front of the historic markers, reading them as if they were stage directions:

> Slowly, over millions of years, crustal pressures
> pushed the seabed skyward. Water, wind, and ice
> attacked the emerging land mass, but the moun-
> tains rose faster than erosion could whittle them
> down. About 40 million years ago, with uplift
> slowing, the Rockies began to waste away.

It had happened before, of course, this failure of memory; it happened to all of them. Even when she was young and start-ing out. Once she was playing Ophelia and craziness seemed natural. She'd stumbled, distracted for a moment, and the oth-ers had filled in. Then she'd garbled her lines, saying "his trousers all unlaced" instead of "his doublet all unbraced," and afterwards they'd rolled about laughing. They said the improvi-sation was better than the original, that she'd improved on Shakespeare. It was the high point of the entire run. They all had these anecdotes; they were part of the repertoire. The youngsters didn't mind; they covered for each other. Hung over, strung out on drugs half the time. Lapses were a joke, not part of anything permanent. They wet their pants at tragic moments, got fits of giggles, broke the props, and took it all in their stride. "I lost it," they said with a shrug. "I freaked."

But lately it had happened more often and caused more problems. Once she was an absent-minded old woman in an Athol Fugard play, and she covered for herself. She put her hands to her head and said she was losing her mind, turning it into an extension of the role, and the young girl playing opposite her immediately caught on.

The Bernhardt play also had a cast of two. They liked that these days; it cut down on costs, not needing to hire more actors. But this time her partner wasn't about to help her out of it. He resented her from the beginning, disliked his role as Sarah's ridiculous secretary, saw himself as a romantic hero. "A deplorable little billy goat of a man," Sarah called Pitou, and that applied to the actor, too. So she never managed to recover from the lapse. Even now she couldn't think of it without wanting to vomit.

It was a longish speech, and she was addressing the ghost of her old admirer: "We are the last of our kind, Oscar Wilde," she said.

At that point each time the wires in Harriet's head crossed, and Lady Bracknell's words floated into her head: "To lose one parent may be regarded as a misfortune; to lose both looks like carelessness."

And after that, nothing. Just an immense silence in her head. Paralysis. And the stupid jerk refused to come to her rescue.

"The last Romantics," the prompter said, and paused. "The last bright banners of ego and happy selfishness."

But it was no good. She couldn't pick up the threads and go on.

Sometimes the real Bernhardt would come onto the stage trembling so badly she could only indicate her gestures. What was behind the histrionics? Were they diversionary tactics dreamed up so that one eccentricity might conceal another?

At dusk Harriet found a bed for the night in a hunting lodge full of the smell of wood smoke. There were Spartan rooms with narrow cots for mountain climbers, for people pitting themselves against nature, testing themselves to the limit, not for tourists who needed bedside tables and lamps so they could read themselves to sleep. She never lingered, taking off at daybreak before anyone else stirred. Sometimes she woke to a dense fog that obliterated everything. She was marooned like an icebreaker in Arctic waters, forced to sit by the window, drinking coffee and watching the mist lift and the mountain return like a dinosaur's back, so close that she could extend her hand and touch it. Then it was time to leave, and she strode out so hurriedly with her actor's gait that onlookers imagined an assignation, a rendezvous.

Bernhardt had tried to orchestrate her death just as she choreographed her life, arranging the *mise en scène*, choosing the hour of her last performance. She kept a coffin always in readiness, even (they said) taking it with her on tours. It was made of rosewood and lined with white satin. She posed in it for the photographers, lighting a tall white candle and holding a sheaf of lilies. "I often think about death," she said, "but only to reassure myself that I shall not die until I am ready."

Bernhardt was full of weaknesses, reckless passions, vanities, affectations, but she turned every liability into a triumph. She travelled with an entourage of sycophants and accumulated a menagerie. She bought cheetahs and monkeys and parrots and turned her household into a circus. What was that but a publicity stunt, something to scandalize the bourgeoisie? Her genius was that she made her antics add to her stature; they didn't leach from it as certain drugs leach calcium from the bones. Her wretched husband and her misbegotten sister were morphine addicts, but Bernhardt herself was abstemious. She even sipped champagne abstemiously, liking the idea better than the taste. If she needed to ease her pain she used the theatre instead of drugs.

When the Duchess of Teck asked how she could bear the strain of acting, Bernhardt said, "*Altesse Royale, je mourrais en scene; c'est mon champ de bataille*" — "I will die on the stage; it is my battlefield." No sordid deaths for her — accidents above the frostline on mountainsides, crumpled cars, rumpled beds, and bottles of pills in cheap hotels, notes scribbled to harrow the survivors.

Harriet would have no survivors; she had to face it: there was no one in whose affections she stood first. She had no children, only an ever-changing troupe of players straight out of drama school; no lover but a series of leading men. She had no home and no family, and she'd never saved a penny. She didn't even have a voice of her own, only a ragbag of hand-me-down phrases from the parts she'd played.

She tried sometimes in the late afternoon to pass the time of day with waiters when restaurants were deserted. "Slow time of day," she'd say, or "Has it been busy?" The question sounded ridiculous, like an operatic soprano attempting a popular song. She had no small talk, could only declaim theatrically in a carrying voice that filled the house.

"May I have ... a refill?"

"Were you an actress?" a waiter asked. The verb tense stabbed her.

Age hadn't stopped Bernhardt. When she was sixty-three, older even than Harriet, she'd given a series of farewell performances, playing Hamlet and the son of Napoleon Bonaparte. Two years later she'd played Joan of Arc. All Paris turned out to laugh at her. But she carried it off triumphantly. The crucial moment came during the scene with the Grand Inquisitor:

"*Quel est ton nom?*"

"*Jeanne.*"

"*Ton age?*"

"*Dix-neuf ans.*"

There was a moment of silence and then the whole house burst into wild applause at the sheer audacity of it. They did the same thing every time she played the scene.

When she was in her seventies, Bernhardt played with one leg amputated, played on and on until she couldn't move across the stage without assistance. But she always managed to seduce the audience, make them fall in love with her over and over again. When she played an aging woman painting her face "in order to repair the irreparable ravages of years," she flung her arms out in a wide appeal and spoke the words softly. The audience gave her a standing ovation, and in response she even managed to stand up, balancing on one leg, hanging on to the throne with one arm, and with the other returning their love.

"The last bright banners of ego and happy selfishness."

"To lose one parent may be regarded as a misfortune; to lose both looks like carelessness."

Bernhardt hadn't lost both parents. She hadn't had two parents to lose. She hadn't even had one. She'd been born to a sixteen-year-old Jewish courtesan, unmarried, of course, who farmed her out at birth. She'd spent the rest of her life making up for that deprivation. And who could blame her? Yet she'd idolized her son and been devoted to her granddaughters. That was love, wasn't it? Round and round went these thoughts in

Harriet's head, and every one brought her back to that moment when her memory had failed and chaos had ensued.

Another morning, another chalet, another lake, another national park. When Harriet stopped at the toll booth to pay, she thought that the altitude and the mountain air were causing her to hallucinate, for her name leaped out at her in bold letters from the notice board beside the window.

"That name," she told the park ranger. "That's my name."

"Do you want to use the phone to call home?" the woman asked pleasantly. "Just pull over." So Harriet drove to the grass verge, left the car, and went inside the little hut.

At first she thought it must be radio work; why would anyone trust her to do more than read from a script? But, no, he assured her it was a "bony fidey" play. The place was a small prairie city, and it was a play by an unknown playwright. His tone was contemptuous. He had the script in front of him and said it wasn't promising. It looked like one of those docudrama things they put on these days about famous couples, but given the circumstances.... He had the title, but he couldn't remember the details.

She didn't need the details; the title told her everything she needed to know. If it had been any other title, she'd have turned it down flat because, even if she didn't mess up, it was humiliating. It was only one step above a play in a church basement put on by the preacher's wife.

"Listen, Harriet, I'm doing you a goddamn favour. Take it or leave it. But I gotta know soon. So don't fuck around. All right, then, by six o'clock tonight. I don't hear and you've lost the part."

The time 'twixt six and now / Must by us both be spent most preciously.

She drove down the main highway looking for a quiet place where the roar of traffic was muted by pine trees. At Red Rock

Canyon, she parked the car and joined a line of people going around the ravine in single file, like ants round a crack in the pavement, falling behind as she pondered the signs:

> The mudstone contains iron. Exposure to the
> air oxidized the iron, like rust on steel, forming
> the red mineral hermalite.

You could hang in bravely to the very end, like those doddering English actors on *Masterpiece Theatre*, too old to remember big parts but doing what were euphemistically called "guest appearances" and "cameo roles"! They were magnificent, their voices still resonant, and they won awards, too, for supporting roles — Lady Bracknell, Lord Marchmain, an elderly missionary in the last days of the Raj.

> The creek is like a giant conveyor belt carrying
> the mountains piece by piece back to the sea.

Should she accept gratefully? Go through the motions with as much dignity as she could muster? Or should she decline proudly — refuse to be put on display as Cleopatra scorned captivity, preferring death? But she knew that death didn't come easily except on the stage. No rockslide would obliterate her, no snake deliver a gentle sleep. It would be impossible to stage a glorious exit.

Six o'clock and here she was back again at the entry to the canyon, almost deserted now save for the animals with motheaten pelts, sickly from being fed junk food by the tourists. She had come full circle and was back at the first sign:

The crumbly bedrock erodes quite rapidly on its own. Unfortunately man hastens this process, as the red rock cannot endure your footsteps. PLEASE STAY ON THE TRAIL AND LET THE CANYON ERODE AT NATURE'S PACE.

Well, then, it was decided. Already her mind was beginning to script a new role. She would walk into the theatre and the buzz in the green room would stop, everyone watching her entry. And it would start up again, the good old backstage gossip, inaccurate, malicious, but infinitely diverting.

"Did you hear about Harriet? My dear, a mountain climber!"

"No! I heard it was a park ranger!"

Back at the toll booth, she placed her call.

"Yes," she said, "yes, I'll do it."

He gave the dates of the audition and said he'd courier the script if she'd just give him an address to send it to. Where the hell was she, anyway?

"Send it to the Lakeshore Hotel."

It was the play's title that had clinched it. It was a name from her childhood, or rather from that imaginary world that had run parallel with it, peopled by extraordinary beings in far-away exotic places. She'd dwelled in that world the way her friends had dwelled in a world of royalty or Hollywood stars. And that world had been orchestrated by one magical being, the only famous person she'd ever come close to knowing and who she came to think of as a distant member of her family, a friend of her Aunt Nina's.

And now, years and years later, when her aunt was gone, the name she hadn't heard for years had been spoken again, conjuring that whole world back into existence. Mazo de la Roche. Surely this was a talisman against disaster if ever there was one.

"She never married," her aunt had said as they looked at a photograph.

"Like you," Harriet said.

"No, not like me, not like me at all," her aunt said.

"Well, what's she like, then?" Harriet said.

"Like nobody you'll ever run across," her aunt said.

II

"Back already?" said the clerk at the desk.

It was ridiculous and made no sense at all. She'd returned to the hotel by the lake in Waterton Park because she'd given its name as the place where she'd receive the script. "Receive," as if it were an immaculate conception and she needed to be in a hallowed place for the event.

"I'm expecting an important package by Federal Express," she said. "Will you let me know the moment it arrives?"

She should have driven to meet it, to pick it up in Lethbridge or Calgary, because the time to prepare was short and the suspense was terrible. But once the decision was made, she felt she'd never been so eager to get her hands on a script before. Well, there was the Bernhardt fiasco; she'd been eager then, too, but it didn't bear thinking about. That way lay madness, and pray god this time would be different.

"Is there a hairdresser around here?" she asked.

"Not one *you'd* want to go to," he said. "For that you'd have to go to Calgary."

She understood from his deferential tone that she was gain-
ing stature already. She'd reasserted herself, regained something,
and had presence once again. While she waited for the script she
paced — along the lakeshore, around the periphery of the town
site, up to the big CPR hotel perched on the headland, where
she carried a drink onto the terrace outside the dining room.
She stared out over the long lake below with mountains encir-
cling it, barely seeing it.

After that summer with her aunt, she'd been like a traveller
who returns from a foreign country with exotic terrain and
strange customs and is disabled by the experience for re-entry
into ordinary, everyday life. It all formed part of a gilded and
mysterious community into which she'd been initiated, and
she would never again be the same person she was before she
went there.

Her family, busy with their own affairs, simply assumed that
she was dissatisfied after living in luxury and being pampered, or
that she was prey to the normal upheavals of adolescence. It
would be nearly a year before she saw her aunt again, and her
only solace was reading. For the rest of the summer she'd
beaten a track to the little public library, where among the
Harlequins and the copies of Gun Digest she'd found what was
necessary to nurture her own private fantasy world.

The script arrived at last. It was not as bulky as she'd
expected, and not so incendiary, either. In fact, the beginning
was pedestrian, like those Shakespearean plays that start off
limping along — two gentlemen conversing, "It wearies
me, you say it wearies you," clumsily setting out the necessary information.

ACT ONE

A publisher's office in Boston. The room is dominated by a large painting of the floating disembodied head of Mazo de la Roche. The publisher, Theodore Speaks, is meticulously dressed in a grey business suit against which his crimson Harvard tie stands out conspicuously. In constrast, the biographer Hamish Donaldson seems frowsy and crumpled.

DON: That's a striking portrait. I'm surprised that your current authors don't resent it.

SPEAKS: Possibly they do. But none of us would be here if it weren't for her. Her books supported the house all through the Depression and the war years.

DON: And yet you're unwilling to publish this story of her life.

SPEAKS: Mr. Donaldson, if I may be perfectly frank, there is no life to be written. She said so herself. "Whatever I am I have put into my books." And there you have it in a nutshell. She wrote books, she lived a quiet life, and she died in her house in Toronto, attended by the sister with whom she spent her life.

DON: Caroline was a cousin and not a sister, wasn't she?

SPEAKS: Sister, cousin, secretary, housekeeper —
            what difference does it make? They were
            two shy Victorian spinsters. They cro-
            cheted. At least the sister did. Made my
            wife a handkerchief once. Very fine work,
            my wife said. She has it still, I believe.

DON: But there were rumours, weren't there?
            One hears stories of unrequited love, bro-
            ken hearts and so on.

SPEAKS: And they were just that. Rumours.

DON: But they were very persistent, weren't they?
            Wasn't Mazo jilted at the altar?

SPEAKS: Come, come, Mr. Donaldson, you're mak-
            ing it all sound like something out of
            Dickens. The mad old woman roaming
            about the ancestral home still in her wed-
            ding gown. All the clocks stopped at the
            very hour of the jilting. I've visited Mazo in
            her home in Toronto and I can assure you
            that was very far from the case.

DON: What about the child?

SPEAKS: Adopted. Antoinette was adopted.

DON: But wasn't it odd for two women in
            advanced middle age to adopt a child?

SPEAKS: Unusual, but certainly not unheard of. In
            fact, a maiden aunt of my own did the very
            same thing.

DON: But couldn't she have been her own
            daughter, born out of wedlock?

SPEAKS: Well, Aunt Augusta was a lively old girl and
            it was said in the family that the girl bore
            an uncanny resemblance to the butler....

DON: No, I don't mean your aunt. I mean Mazo.

SPEAKS: (laughing) Oh, Mazo? Was the daughter
            hers? Not a chance in hell.

DON: Why ever not?

SPEAKS: Mr. Donaldson, you never met Mazo. She
            was, how shall I say it, not a womanly
            woman. She was masculine, or sexless, rather.
            Certainly not attractive to the opposite sex
            ... not the type to appeal to a man at all.

DON: But tastes do vary in these matters.

SPEAKS: Do they, Mr. Donaldson? May I say some-
            thing, man to man, and with no offence
            intended? It seems to me that your natural
            inclination is towards the novel form. The
            Gothic novel. And, as someone with a good

sense of the current publishing scene, I have to say that the market in costume Gothics has never been better. It's always brisk. Much better, in fact, than the market in biography — unless you have a sensational life, with some bizarre forms of sexuality. That always sells, of course. But my advice to you, my dear fellow, is to try your hand at a novel. Or a play.

DON: Maybe someday. But at the moment, Mazo has her teeth in me. She's cast a spell on me somehow, and I can't shake it. When I read her novels I feel there must be a story behind them, a story in the person who wrote them. They're the novels of someone with a fund of experience, someone who understands — well — passion, sensuality, adventure.

SPEAKS: I'm a Harvard man myself, Donaldson, and inclined more to restraint than to colourful judgements.

DON: I keep coming back to the rumours that were never put to rest. The child, for example. You say she couldn't have been Mazo's. What about Caroline? Did she appeal to men? Was she attractive?

SPEAKS: Caroline? Oh very. Oh, yes indeed. In fact, I —

DON: Well, there you are. Surely she holds the key to everything?

SPEAKS: She holds the key to everything, but she won't let anyone near the door. She's very secretive. Even more secretive than Mazo. And besides, she sees almost no one.

DON: Except the daughter?

SPEAKS: Perhaps not even her. Antoinette was estranged from Mazo for years. It's always just been Mazo and Caroline.

DON: Mazo and Caroline.

SPEAKS: It's Caro-*line*, by the way, not Caro-*lyn*. Mazo had a very particular way of pronouncing it, as if she wanted to hang on to every syllable. Caro — LINE. I can hear her now, calling out the name with that special inflection she had — Car-O-line. Car-O-line.

"You seem to be very interested in this Mazo de la Roche," the librarian said one day as she stamped Harriet's book for the umpteenth time. "Is she any good?"

"It's not Mazzo, it's May-zo," Harriet said before she could catch herself.

"My," said the librarian, "you are well informed, aren't you? And how did you know that?"

"My aunt Nina told me," Harriet said. What she really wanted to say was "My aunt knows her," but that would have been showing off, and besides it was not strictly true. Her aunt didn't actually know Mazo, she just knew all about her. Harriet had almost the same conversation with her English teacher in school. But unlike the librarian, the English teacher had read some of Mazo's books. She said she liked them on the whole but she had "some reservations."

"Oh, like what?" Harriet asked.

"A bit too much sex," the teacher said, looking first to the left and then to the right and lowering her voice.

Her aunt finally arrived the next spring bringing presents for all of them. She brought Harriet some new clothes and Mazo's latest book. It was called *Variable Winds at Jalna*. There weren't many opportunities for Harriet to be alone with her aunt, the odd stroll around the neighbourhood or to the corner grocery store, but whenever she could shake off her sister and her mother, she plied her aunt with questions about Mazo and Caroline and their daughter, Antoinette. They had now sold the mansion in England and lived in a big house outside Toronto. Mazo and Caroline had made a trip out to Vancouver, but Antoinette hadn't come with them because she was in boarding school. Her aunt answered her questions thoughtfully and seriously, as if the subject was just as important to her as it was to Harriet. They discussed boarding school, both of them agreeing that Antoinette probably enjoyed being with girls her own age, and speculating about the sports she might play. Harriet, who had read lots of stories about boarding schools, thought she probably played lacrosse.

And then quite suddenly it all ended. Harriet, scheming to be alone with her aunt and often sneaking into the bedroom she'd been obliged to vacate to make room for her, hadn't been monitoring the barometric pressure of tension in the house. And so she was oblivious to the growing storm between her mother and her aunt until it finally erupted.

Her aunt's present to her father was a bottle of Scotch whisky, and she usually joined him for a glass of it after they'd had their supper. The bottle sat on the sideboard all day, and her mother scowled at it every time she dusted. Harriet could still see the label — Mortlach — because it was the same name as a small town on the highway that they passed on their way to Swift Current. When the row broke out, it had something to do with the Mortlach, and something to do with the book her aunt had brought her. It began innocently enough, all of them sitting around the living room, her dad and her aunt on the sofa with their glasses of whisky, and Harriet herself sitting on the floor beside them with *Variable Winds at Jalna* on her lap. Her mother looked up from her knitting and said she was doing so much reading she was going to put her eyes out if she didn't look out and end up wearing glasses.

"Reading won't do her any harm," said her aunt, who usually avoided contradicting her mother. "In fact, it will help her with her education."

"What education?" her mother said.

"There's no reason she shouldn't go to college," her aunt said. "She's smart enough."

"She sure is," her dad said, smiling at her. "She'd make a good teacher."

"And what's the use of going to college for three or four years," her mother said, "when all she's going to do at the end of it is get married? Waste of time and money, if you ask me."

"Even if she does, it's good to have something to fall back on," her aunt said.

"Well, let's hope she'll behave herself, then she won't need anything to fall back on," her mother said pointedly.

"Oh, right, it slipped my mind. Getting married will provide her with everything she wants, just like it did you." And her aunt looked around the room, dusting every shabby piece of furniture deliberately with her eyes. Even Harriet, listening in alarm, thought she'd gone too far this time.

And she had; that was the last of the yearly visits. The next morning her aunt packed her bags, refused her dad's offer of a ride to the airport, called a taxi, and left even before she'd had her breakfast. She still sent presents at Christmas and remembered Harriet's birthday, and about twice a year she called up and talked to her on the phone.

Eventually Harriet got over the disappearance of her aunt from her life, just as she got over her obsession with Mazo and her daughter, but like most childhood obsessions it was reactivated periodically throughout her life. It was odd that, although she wasn't a reader of newspapers and magazines, she always seemed to stumble on articles about Mazo. When she did, they drew her back for a time into the world she'd inhabited for those two formative years in her young life.

There were always tattered copies of *Chatelaine* lying around backstage, and once she came across a back issue that had fallen open at a spread of pictures of Mazo and her home. It wasn't one of the great houses that Harriet remembered from the photograph albums her aunt had shown her, but a mansion in Ontario with stables and an old carriage house that served as a garage. Mazo was sitting on the lawn in front of the house in a wicker chair, with two dogs lying on the grass beside her, and smiling up at her daughter, who was handing her a sheaf of papers. Antoinette was wearing a summer dress, and they looked odd together — an old woman and a young girl. The picture seemed posed somehow, and they seemed stiff and awkward.

Harriet had been down east playing summer stock when Mazo's death was announced. This time the name jumped out at her in headlines from the newspaper stand: "Mazo de la Roche Dead at 82" and "Famous Author Dies." She bought all the papers and learned the details of the funeral at the Anglican Cathedral in Toronto. She was near enough to make it there and back in a day, and for one brief moment she'd thought of making up a pretext, giving her young understudy a break, and catching the train into the city. She could have taken a taxi at Union Station and joined the throng of mourners, like any other fan. She'd have finally gotten to see Antoinette and Caroline, though she thought they would probably be veiled like queens following the cortège of a dead monarch. But she hadn't gone after all, though at the appointed hour she'd drifted into a trance and been there in spirit, and for days afterwards she was abstracted and dreamy.

Harriet had entered many strange places in her life; it was what she did when she prepared for a part — Lady Macbeth's Scotland, Cleopatra's Egypt, Saint Joan's Rouen, Sarah Bernhardt's Paris — but the summer she visited her aunt had been the beginning, the first of those imaginary countries. So there was congruence in having this play offered to her at the end of her career, as if a circle had miraculously closed and her own people had come to reclaim her. Not only that, but it finally lifted the screen away from Mazo's mysterious world and revealed all the secrets that lay behind it.

MAZO: Caroline, do you remember when you almost went off that time with … that man?

CARO: Of course, I remember. It was a very long time ago.

MAZO: You didn't love him, did you?

CARO: Of course not, Mazo.

MAZO: Darling, did you want so much to be a wife?

CARO: Is that so very strange for a young girl? I wanted to have a home of my own, away from the family, away from your mother and Aunt Eva.

MAZO: I want to marry you, Caroline, so that you can never, ever decide to leave again.

CARO: So this is what all this restlessness is about?

MAZO: The danger of almost losing you haunts me still. And now with this job you'll be meeting people. Men, Caroline. I want them to know that you belong to me. I want a wedding in a church. I want a marriage certificate. I want to see you wearing a band of gold on your finger. I want you to say things like "thereto I plight thee my troth," and I want to say "with all my worldly goods I thee endow."

CARO: But, darling, you don't have any worldly goods. That's why I've taken this job.

MAZO: Oh, Caroline, why not?

CARO: To put it bluntly, your late father was not much of a provider and no one else is going to provide for us.

MAZO: I don't mean *that*. I mean why can't we be married? Why can't two people who love each other as we do and plan to share everything and each other and live together for the rest of their lives....

She read on, transfixed, and what she read confirmed what she'd known all along, only she'd never actually put it into words. She fell asleep with the words going round and round in her head.

III

It was always the same with auditions. Because she was tense she drank too much, and the drinking only increased the tension and aggravated all the other problems — stiffness in the limbs, the inability to move gracefully and think clearly.

She woke up with a hangover and a panic attack, thinking for a moment she was in a motel room in the mountains, still in flight. But no, she was in a rooming house in a small prairie city. The room was shabby, verging on squalid — a torn curtain in the window, horrendous wallpaper with great feathers of some kind. She tried to figure out what they were. Fleurs-de-lys? Fans for dancing girls? Plumed pens for wedding guests? Just thinking about them made her stomach churn.

More familiar items stood on the rickety bamboo table beside the bed. A crumpled script, a bottle of Scotch with the level ominously low, and the tattered paperbacks that were her bibles — upbeat theatrical autobiographies with catchy titles and depressing biographies of celebrated actors. She craved coffee and cigarettes but knew she'd have to settle for aspirin and a cold shower with someone pounding on the bathroom door before she was halfway through.

The stress was proportional to the desire for the part, and in this case the desire was high. If she didn't succeed she'd be relegated to the ranks of backstage workers, that army of dressmakers, builders of sets, painters of scenery, arrangers of wires and lighting. They called themselves artists — makeup artists, costume artists — but they were really just technicians. Everyone knew who the artists were, the only ones who really counted. It was the actors who had all the responsibility for the success or failure, for the livelihood and continuation of the whole lot of them. And they came together, the actors, a cabal bound together by that knowledge. They fired each other up, growing together, sometimes intensely, living and even sleeping together. And no one minded — all was permitted and justified by the importance of the play and the enormous responsibility they carried on their shoulders. They were apart from the world, with their own times and seasons like lovers, sleeping through the mornings, coming alive at dusk, the alertness lasting beyond the midnight hours, sometimes to daybreak. They were the aristocrats of this ragtag world, the others merely servants, bit players, like the spear carriers and the attendant lords.

It all built up to the grand climax of the first night. After that, if it went well, the momentum was sustained for the entire run. But already after the first night there was the imminence of death. The certainty of doom fanned the intensity. And when it came the ending was terrible, the final curtain like the start of a funeral, followed by partings, goodbyes, the diaspora, departures at the bus station for different cities. You wanted to die. You did die. You were dead in every way that really mattered, buried alive, a pulse ticking faintly like the beat of a failing heart. A frog buried in mud.

If you were lucky, it began again. Often it did. Slowly at first, you roused yourself. Another script, another cast of players. It was pale compared with the last one, a distraction merely, something to pass the time, to help you through the half-life you were living, the twilight world you inhabited. Everything in it was gross and thick — the words, the sets, and the leading man, a great oaf with bad breath who trod on your feet.

And then quite suddenly it started all over again. Perhaps at one rehearsal, unexpectedly, the magic started to happen. You left the theatre in a dazzle of joy, knowing that it was going to be even better than it was last time, the best it had ever been. Life had returned as surely as the sap rising in the trees in springtime, as the incoming tide of the ocean, proving that it would do so forever. The oaf turned out to be a prince. But it had been touch and go for a while, and you'd died before you were born again.

But if it didn't start over again — if the parts dried up and the offers never came — then you entered the valley of the shadow of death. Perhaps you would end up sitting with other old women sewing beads on costumes and exchanging gossip about who was with whom, who was drinking or on drugs, who was on the way up to movies or on the way down to television commercials. There were always jobs for superannuated actresses. They could star in advertisements for medicine to cure hemorrhoids and vaginal dryness — giving such credence to the indecencies of old age that they became permanently associated with them. And if you couldn't face that you could retire from the stage altogether. You could be a receptionist in a dentist's office or a hostess in a restaurant.

All that stands between me and those horrors is this part as Mazo de la Roche, thought Harriet as she made her way to the theatre in driving rain, on foot because she had turned in the rent-a-wreck the day before. It was bad for the farmers at this time of year. *Bad for everyone*, she thought as she turned her collar up and ducked her head against the downpour.

There was the usual mob in the foyer, people clustered around the coffee machine, grabbing donuts, catching up on the gossip. She filled a Styrofoam cup at the machine and leaned against the wall studying the competition. Jane Merritt stood out with her impressive height and red hair, the local girl who had made good — gone to RADA, returned to Stratford, done film — a star! There'd been a great high school teacher in this town, and he'd fostered a whole group of star-struck youngsters who became actors. They hung together now, screeching like the latest arrivals at a family reunion. But why was Jane Merritt here? Had something fallen apart for her too?

Then someone jogged Harriet's elbow so sharply that the hot coffee jumped out of its cup.

"Harriet! Great haircut!" (True, the Calgary haircut had been a sound investment.)

"Brandi! I thought you were down east."

Well at least she had one ally, one friend. They'd teamed up numerous times and never had a bad word for each other. Hermia and Helena, Gwendolyn and Cicely. Even Goneril and Reagan once. With Brandi it was always casting against type. Because she was fair and petite she got traditional female roles, though in fact she was rough, tough, and foul-mouthed. Recently she'd got work with a movie outfit in the maritimes.

"I was. Couldn't stand the fucking sea, though. It was full of body parts from that air crash."

"It didn't work out for you down there?" Harriet said.

"Yeah. Good pay. Terrific, in fact, but I need to be here. The old man's about to croak. Fucking lung cancer."

"I'm sorry."

"Yeah, well. What about you? What brought you back to this asshole of nowhere?"

"I want this part badly, but I don't suppose I've much of a chance." She nodded towards Jane Merritt, who was surrounded by a group of admirers.

"Old ginger bush! She isn't really interested, just here to see the folks and stir up the fan club. She's waiting on two movie offers and she'll cut out of this if she gets one. Let's tank up before it starts."

Harriet sat next to Brandi, needing coffee but afraid to drink so much that she'd have to pee every five minutes, waiting for her turn, watching the others, two men going first. Brandi whispered a joke about a brain transplant patient wanting to know why women's brains were half price.

"It's not their fault," Harriet whispered back. "It's the play, it's still raw in places." She felt sorry for the men, lads really, trying to make something of the pedestrian script.

DON: Can you tell me what she was like when you first met her thirty years ago?

SPEAKS: She was well into middle age by then.

DON: But didn't you get a sense of her early life?

SPEAKS: The facts are well known. Caroline was an orphan, taken in by Mazo's family. They grew up from childhood together. Lived in the family home until Mazo's parents died. I'll tell you one thing...

DON: Yes?

SPEAKS: They were well-connected. Came from one of the best families in that part of the world.

DON: But I understand they grew up on the bare bones of privation.

SPEAKS: I didn't say they had material wealth. I said they came from a good family. Good breeding. There's a difference. Perhaps you have to be a New Englander to understand the distinction.

DON: Are you sure? I mean about the family?

SPEAKS: I'm a pretty fair judge in these matters. And my wife would confirm my judgement. They came to Boston once, and she threw a party for them. Invited all her friends, some of the very oldest New England families. She told me the gals were perfectly at ease. And that was my own observation when I visited their house.

DON: Oh yes?

SPEAKS: Well, the way they handled the servants for one thing. They had a large staff. But thoroughly unobtrusive. They brooked no insubordination or familiarity. And they treated them like old retainers who'd been in the family for generations.

DON: They did?

SPEAKS: Called up one time in a great state. They'd had to dismiss the chauffeur and wanted to make sure he was well taken care of. Anyone else would have thrown him out on his heels. But not them. Placed him with a friend of mine, as a matter of fact.

DON: What had he done?

SPEAKS: I never knew, exactly. Some minor infraction. Probably called one of them by her first name. But that's what I mean — the personal concern. And yet the rectitude. That's a sure sign of breeding.

DON: Is it?

SPEAKS: And the house, too. Good old furniture. Good paintings. Good art. Nothing showy, nothing vulgar. No hint of the nouveau riche, of antique dealers or decorators. Solid taste. Absolutely unerring taste. You don't learn that kind of thing, Donaldson. And it doesn't happen overnight. It's bred into one. Over several generations.

There was a general stirring and buzz and movement to the coffee machine at the end of the scene.

"What the fuck!" said Brandi to Harriet as she came back from the bathroom. "Do we need work this badly?"

"It'll get whipped into shape," said Harriet.

"Yeah. Before it moves to the big cities without us. Well, here goes." And she went off to read a scene with Jane Merritt. It featured Mazo as a young girl, and Merritt was plausible. They were both so good they could have been reading the *Financial Post* and it would have come alive. And the painful part to Harriet was that they worked so well together.

MAZO: When the rain stops, the air will be fresh again and we can go for a walk. We'll go by the Mansion and see what the Masseys are doing.

CARO: Mazo, the high point of my life is not peeping at the Masseys.

MAZO: You enjoy it as much as I do.

CARO: Oh yes. What do we have on our calendar today? Why the Masseys are having a party forsooth. We can pretend to be taking a stroll down Jarvis Street so we can watch the fine ladies being helped from their carriages. Perhaps one will toss us a coin and we can grovel for it.

MAZO: Caroline, please don't. Father will find a job soon and things will get better.

CARO: And if he does, do you really think it will last longer than any of the others? And we don't have the rent for another month in this place even. You heard them at supper last night. We have to move again. This time down by the railroad tracks. Well, they can move without me.

MAZO: Will it be any better to work for strangers? To wait tables and smile and earn tips. At least we're family and took you in when no one else did....

CARO: I think I've paid off that debt several times in my ten years as errand girl and beast of burden. My god, they can't even call me by my first name. It's "Clemmie, do this! Clemmie, do that!"

MAZO: They call me Maisie and I hate it just as much.

CARO: Well, they won't be calling me anything for a very long time if I can help it. And I won't be waiting tables forever.

MAZO: Not the innkeeper's son. Oh, you aren't thinking of marrying him, are you?

CARO: I shall be free to lead my own life and do whatever I wish.

MAZO: But getting married isn't leading your own life. It's leading someone else's.

CARO: True. But since they never let me go to school, it's the only prospect I have.

MAZO: The prospect of being an innkeeper's wife in Newmarket?

CARO: Is that so different from being an unpaid servant in Cawthra Square?

MAZO: There are different kinds of servitude, Caroline.

CARO: In that case there's something to be said for varying them.

MAZO: Caroline, this house depresses me as much as it depresses you. I feel like a changeling, dropped by an accident of birth into a roach's nest. Those nights when I wake you with my screaming — do you know what my nightmare is? I dream I'm tied down and being overrun by roaches, nasty little insects, coming out from all their corners in droves. I believe I knew from the very moment I was born that I wasn't a Roach. All I ever dreamed of was getting away.

It went on and on as if, in spite of the script, the acting brought the situation to life and everyone watching was caught up in it and enthralled. So it seemed that a good half-hour went by before the director finally clapped her hands and said, "Thank you."

By the time Harriet was called up, the crowd had thinned out as those whose turns were over drifted away. She was sure that Jane Merritt and Brandi had the parts. Meg Wagstaff, who was to play Caroline to Harriet's Mazo, was hopeless, over-weight, and gross in every way. Harriet felt she was much too old for Mazo and sure that together they would make a farce of the scene.

> CARO: If one of us gets away, she can rescue the other. We don't have to be separated. When I'm married you can come with me to Newmarket.

> MAZO: I was born in that godforsaken town and I've no desire to return — ever. And I don't want to be a guest in your home, a hanger-on, a maiden aunt, bossing the children about. I don't want to share you, Caroline. I want you all to myself. I need you, Caroline.

CARO: But I'm tired of being needed. I want to need someone else for a change.

MAZO: But don't you need me? Haven't I taken care of you since you were seven years old? Didn't I play with you and amuse you and make you happy even in the worst of times?

CARO: Darling, you did. But I'm not a child any longer. I'm a woman and I need to escape this family.

MAZO: Oh Caroline, there's a way we can escape even if we never leave this house, as long as we stay together.

CARO: (gently) Mazo, we're too old for your play. We're women of marriageable age. I'll be twenty in a few more years. And I'm going to be married. Even if I have to wait on tables, at least I shall be called by my first name.

MAZO: If you leave, I shall die. That's all. It will be the end of me.

CARO: Nonsense. You have so much talent and so much imagination — you can do anything.

MAZO: But what can a woman do, Caroline, except get married? You said so yourself. And I won't get married. I've never been interested in a man in my whole life. I'm different from you. And I can't do my play by myself. Oh Caroline, don't abandon our play.

CARO: Darling, we can't plan our entire lives around dressing up and acting out a play in a dark bedroom.

MAZO: We can't, Caroline? Why can't we? Isn't it better than anything we've ever done? Hasn't everything else seemed pale in comparison? It's our own private world over which we have complete control. And in it we can be anyone we like. We can stop being Clemmie and Maisie — you're not Clemmie, or even Caroline Clement. You were Alayne Archer, and now that you are married to Eden Whiteoak you are Alayne Whiteoak. Who are you?

CARO: I'm Alayne … Alayne Whiteoak. And I'm finding living in the Ontario countryside a little strange after New York. I stroll around the grounds of Whiteoak Manor trying to feel at home.

MAZO: So, my brother Eden's lovely wife is out for an afternoon stroll.

CARO: Renny, I would rather walk alone.

MAZO: Alayne, don't you think that brother-in-law
          and sister-in-law should be friends? We
          both love the same person, and so it follows
          as a matter of course that we should love
          each other.

CARO: Renny, your attentions trouble me. There's
          an undercurrent in everything you say and
          do. I would rather you kept a distance from
          me —

"Thank you, thank you," a handclap, and it was over. Harriet felt totally humiliated. Brandi's droll, sympathetic expression said it all.

"Do you want to go out for a drink or something?" Harriet asked.

"Can't, I'm sorry," Brandi said. "I'm supposed to be at a fucking death watch."

"Well, that's what I was inviting you to," Harriet said.

"Another time," Brandi said. "Hey, maybe I'll come in on Sunday and we can look at houses together."

"What houses?" Harriet said.

"That's the prescribed Sunday afternoon entertainment in this burg," Brandi said. "Garage sales on Saturday and open houses courtesy of the real estate agents on Sunday. Have you forgotten? You grew up here, didn't you?"

"Sort of," said Harriet. "It's been a long time, though. And I'll probably be leaving in a day or two."

"Hey, don't sweat it," Brandi said. "You're a fucking shoo-in for the part."

IV

The town was familiar to her. She knew every heaving flagstone, every crack in the pavement in the grid of streets she'd walked day after day on her way to school, her perspective on it altering as she herself changed. In the beginning it was a celestial city whose core drew her downtown every Saturday afternoon. Then, after journeys to other cities, it dwindled to a rundown prairie town battered by the ordeal of its long, hard winter.

It was a schizophrenic town, leafy and full of flowers in the long summer days, ripe and mellow in the early fall when the smoky smell of distant forest fires mingled with the smell of fruit. Then, abruptly, sometimes overnight, the curtain came down on the pleasant sunny scene. When it rose again, the place was unrecognizable, transformed into a windswept settlement on the edge of Antarctica, almost uninhabitable. And there was no entr'acte. Spring was elided between the two extremes, the long, Lenten season of penitence culminating in no climactic resurrection. The drama was episodic and continual, consisting of daily ordeals of blizzard and ice.

For a long time it had existed only as the backdrop to her childhood recollections, and now she had stepped back into it. Whatever happened with the play, it was a homecoming of sorts. She hailed the surviving landmarks, finding them dearly familiar in spite of changes, like relatives rejuvenated by crude facelifts, and she mourned those obliterated to make way for new buildings.

In place of the old buildings there were skyscrapers — glass, metal, and air-conditioned — banks and sterile office buildings with institutional artworks in the foyer intended (presumably) to uplift the soul, but in fact constituting a silent rebuke. Several had cows, either depicted in paintings or sculpted life-size in bronze. There seemed to be an infestation of these domestic animals, perhaps because they too were going the way of the buffalo and were on the verge of extinction.

Among the disappeared were the fur stores, the corner groceries, and the cafés with their snakeweed plants, fly-specked oilcloth tables, and clientele of good old boys. Gone was the old Capitol Theatre, where she had lined up on Saturday afternoons, tantalized by the framed stills of movies she would never get to see and which seemed all the more alluring for that.

Yet in spite of the encroachment, and in spite of two downtown malls linked by a food court, the centre held. This was a town with a centre. There was a square park with a war memorial at the point where paths intersected, a statue of Sir John A. Macdonald, a children's playground, triangles of grass, and a few flowerbeds. Around its periphery stood the churches of various uncompromising, ununited denominations — the Anglican cathedral, the First Baptist, Knox Metropolitan. There was a library, too, a modern building with ramps for wheelchairs, and — dominating the whole — the old CPR hotel, which in spite of periodic facelifts remained its inimitable self, resistant to change or disguise. Solid, steady, and dignified with its spacious foyer and high ceilings, a living reproach to newer hotels with waterslides, chlorinated pools, and exercise rooms. It was a poor relation of similar buildings across the country — the Empress, the Banff Springs, the Chateau Laurier — but on a smaller scale as befitted its humbler setting, yet nevertheless deserving of the Homeric epithet "venerable."

The theatre — The Globe — was housed in the former city hall, the last holdout of an earlier era, testimony to the human spirit not entirely quenched by commerce and technology, dwarfed and crowded though it was by bank buildings. On the ground floor, in defiance of the conspiracies of consumerism, a repairer of watches, the Tic Doc, had a small booth, and nearby a repairer of shoes for those who still wore out heels and soles by walking. One of the theatre's side doors opened onto a pedestrian mall, a pleasant place with a few trees bravely planted at regular intervals in squares of unpaved earth. Vestiges of human creativity clustered about the theatre as if they had taken heart from its survival. There were two bookstores, a music store, and a hole-in-the-wall with a wide range of papers and magazines, and pornography in the back.

The rain had stopped, and Harriet walked out into the carnival atmosphere, recognizing the heady enjoyment that prevails on fine days in a cold climate. Buskers and street vendors and artists of all kinds drew the workers down from their cubicles in the high-rise buildings to linger in the open air.

She was arrested immediately by the spectacle of a mime with a white face and white gloved hands holding a pose on a small platform, arms outstretched, still as a statue. Passers-by paused more often in front of him than any of the others, a small crowd gathering to stand subdued as if his immobility were contagious. A Greek fisherman's hat, identical to the one on his head, lay on the pavement garnering more coins than his competitors. When she stooped to put in her coins, Harriet noticed a healthy number of folded bills.

Moving along she passed a wooden cart, elegantly and skilfully painted with red Georgia O'Keefe poppies and emblazoned with the words "Carte Blanche." From it a young woman dispensed drinks and sandwiches and carried on several bantering conversations at once. The people swarmed the cart and hung around much longer than the acquisition of food and drink warranted. For a moment, drawn by the poppies, Harriet thought of patronizing the cart but settled instead for indoor seating and quiet. The lunch crowd was thinning, the workers already drifting back to their cages, when Harriet ducked into a nearby restaurant where the tables were littered with debris and the waiters showed signs of battle fatigue. Only one table was still occupied — by four women obviously not part of the nine-to-five work force, and yet not housewives. They were talking animatedly, an empty litre carafe of white wine on the table. Naturally the waiters were not about to hurry over to a single woman, looking dazed and wanting only a cup of coffee and a place to sit.

"May I join you?"

The woman who wrote the play plumped into the chair opposite Harriet without waiting for an answer.

"I saw you come in and thought we'd better get acquainted. Hope Prince."

She could have been Harriet's age, perhaps younger, perhaps older; it was hard to tell. She had the air of a precocious child and spoke with an English accent.

"Do you mind the smoking section?" Harriet asked.

Hope ignored the question. Harriet would eventually get used to this, Hope's tendency to ignore remarks that deflected the conversation from her *idée fixe*. She was almost ruthlessly focused.

"I saw your Sarah Bernhardt. I thought you were terrific. Saw it twice, in fact."

"Oh." Harriet flinched visibly.

"Don't worry. I feel the same way when people say they've read something I've written," said Hope, as if she read her mind. "Exposed."

Harriet wondered if she should know what this woman had written and return the compliment.

"That's one of the reasons I wanted you so badly for Mazo."

Fireworks went off in Harriet's mind as words and phrases connected — *I thought we'd better get acquainted*; *I wanted you for Mazo*. Of course; she'd known all along it wasn't an agent's sentimental fondness that got the script rushed out to her.

By now the four women were at the stage of divvying up the bill, rooting about in their purses for the tip. The jingle attracted a waiter to their corner so that he managed to take their orders without much effort.

"Grilled cheese. Caesar salad. Perrier," Hope said so decisively that Harriet ordered the same. One of the four women came to the table to ask Hope how the play was going along, and Hope asked her how her own play was going.

"Second act problems," the woman said. "Usual thing."

Hope nodded sympathetically and introduced Harriet.

"She's our Mazo," she said.

"I saw you in something," the woman said. "Sarah Bernhardt." They all knew, of course they did. If they hadn't been present for the debacle, they must have heard about it.

"What about Jane Merritt?" Harriet asked after the woman left.

"Too big a fish for this small pond."

"Oh," said Harriet, deflated even more. "Meaning she'd make the rest of us look like amateur night in the church basement?"

"And hard to handle. And she has other fish to fry. She's hoping for a part in a movie with Dustin Hoffman. *And* she's not altogether reliable."

Not altogether reliable, thought Harriet, looking at the shrewd eyes swimming like fishes behind the thick lenses.

"And what about you? This is very different from Bernhardt!" Hope said.

"It's a long story. I've been interested in Mazo since I read her as a kid."

"Oh?" It was an invitation to say more.

"Well, there was a family connection in a way. My aunt worked for Mazo's cousin ... so I felt she was in the family, the nearest I'd ever come to a real writer. And you? Did you read all the books when you were a kid?"

"No. They were popular in England, but I missed out on them somehow. I found them much later, and since I did I've gone through various stages — reading her, writing about her, researching her life, teaching her...."

"Teaching?"

"It's my day job. I teach at the university."

"But Mazo isn't the kind of thing you teach, is it? I thought —"

"She was beyond the pale. The last mourner for the waning influence of the British Empire in Canada, the provider of pulp fiction for frustrated housewives."

"So your project is one of rehabilitation?"

"In the beginning it was. I have to admit I'm evangelical by nature, but the consuming interest became something else."

"The secrets?"

"If you mean all those narrative hooks I put in the opening scene — the love affair with Caroline, where the daughter came from, the fabrication of the aristocratic background — no! It was none of those, although they were part of it."

Harriet waited.

"It was how anyone so out of sync with the real world could lead her own inner life, keep it absolutely intact, and yet appear before the world in a disguise that made her completely — or almost completely — acceptable. She didn't just 'pass,' as someone of a different race might pass, but she led a double life, and she twisted that other life into fictional currency and used it to conquer the world. It was an incredible feat."

Harriet tried to absorb Hope's explanation.

"This will all become clear during the course of the play," Hope said in a tone that signalled the subject was closed for the moment.

Suddenly Harriet knew who Hope reminded her of — her high school English teacher.

"Yes, yes," said Hope with a grimace, "it's my fate to remind everybody of their high school English teacher."

She was applying herself to the food in front of her, eating the salad with her fingers and cutting up the sandwich into small pieces — the eccentric eating habits of someone who lives alone. Harriet began to warm towards her.

"It's a compliment," said Harriet. "She was wonderful. One of the reasons I went into the theatre. She had us learning masses of poetry. Passages from Shakespeare, the sonnets, sonnets by Milton and Wordsworth and Keats and lots more. I can still remember them. She had a wonderful voice. There are whole passages of Shakespeare that I still hear in her voice."

"Ah yes. That's what they said of Edith Evans. When she spoke a line, you heard it ever afterwards in her voice. But your English teacher probably had years of elocution lessons. We all did."

"Oh really?" said Harriet, interested because she really hadn't known what she'd been heir to.

"Well, those of us who came from Lancashire and Yorkshire or other benighted places and went to grammar schools. If we were headed to university, the first requirement for fitting into mainstream society was to shed our northern accents. And in the process of acquiring this verbal camouflage we learned so much poetry that it set us up for life."

"It did?"

"All that rote-learning spawned a whole generation of good writers. Nothing like getting the cadences of the great poets — or even the third-rate ones — imprinted subliminally on your developing brain. Beats television commercials any day. So naturally we became English teachers, and, not wanting to be rendered back to our northern habitats, many of us skipped across the ocean and offered our talents to the New World."

A certain inflection in her voice made Harriet wonder if she was serious.

"I'm afraid those talents weren't much appreciated," Harriet said, "at least not in my school. The parents complained that there was too much parroting of useless stuff and not enough thinking."

"So they put a stop to the rote-learning, and you didn't do a whole lot of thinking, either. And that created a great vacuum that provided fertile ground for all kinds of mischief. But you managed to slip in just under the wire and learn something useful. And that set *you* up for life."

"Perhaps it did," said Harriet, somewhat surprised to see her high school education summed up in such a way.

"It was the same all over," Hope said. "I taught high school when the conventional wisdom was that knowing your subject didn't mean you knew how to teach. So expertise in your subject became a liability. Meanwhile, learning how to teach, like learning how to be a good parent, remained elusive. Schools of education flourished, and high schools grew weaker. It was the beginning of a downward slide. Luckily, I jumped off the merry-go-round and hopped over to the university."

"Just like that?"

"Well, it wasn't quite that simple. There was the small matter of a couple of extra degrees that I had to acquire."

"Were they worth the effort?"

"In some ways. You don't have parents on your back, you have a certain amount of autonomy, and scholarly expertise still counts for something. But the same forces that eroded the high schools are now working on the universities — at least in the humanities. It's a long story, Harriet. But as we're still functioning, I'd like you to come and talk to one of my classes."

"Be glad to," Harriet said, although it was the last thing she wanted to do.

"But getting back to Mazo?"

"That's a long story too," said Harriet. They gathered their things together and emerged into the mall, then, discovering that they were going in the same direction, they walked across the park together.

The mime and most of the buskers had disappeared. The pictures drawn by the pavement artists remained, and the white cart was deserted, its owner packing up for the day. She waved cheerfully at Hope.

"Hi, Blanche!" said Hope. "Got any of those hashish bars?"

"Sure," said Blanche, laughing. "I kept them back for you."

"This is Harriet, the lead in the play," Hope said.

"Wow!"

"One of my former students," Hope said. Harriet would conclude eventually that the entire population of the city consisted of Hope's former students.

"Is Blanche her real name?" Harriet asked, looking at the elaborate lettering of "Carte Blanche" in its circle of Georgia O' Keefe poppies.

"Has been for as long as I've known her," Hope said. "But I don't know if the name or the vocation came first."

"It's hardly a vocation, is it?" said Harriet.

"For her it seems to be. She takes it very seriously," Hope said, adding in her opinionated way, "Names can influence the directions lives take."

Harriet was about to ask Hope if her name made her preternaturally optimistic when they arrived outside Harriet's rooming house. It was a white frame house, with an old sofa on the porch sprouting coiled wire springs and stuffing. Loud music blared out of one of the upstairs windows, and a compost heap at the side of the house was releasing a truly horrible smell.

"The usual foul and pestilent congregation of vapours," said Hope, as if she was familiar with the place. "Not a very peaceable kingdom."

"True," said Harriet. "I'll probably move soon."

"I have a house on the crescents," Hope said. "I often let the top floor to a student. It just so happens that it's vacant at the moment."

"I'm more or less committed," Harriet said. "I have an aunt in town."

The excuse was the knee-jerk reaction of someone who leads an irregular life, needs freedom, and doesn't want anyone taking note of her comings and goings or counting the bottles in the garbage. But even without that, the idea of living under the scrutiny of those shrewd eyes would have been too much.

"That isn't the aunt who knew Mazo?"

"No, she died. This is another one."

"Well, we must get together and talk about our shared obsession," Hope said. "You must come and see my collection of photographs of Mazo and Caroline."

"I have some photographs of them too," Harriet said, "if I can only find them."

"Passed on by your aunt?"

"No," Harriet said. "As a matter of fact, I stole them."

It seemed from the dilation of the eyes behind the glasses that an explanation was necessary.

"I stayed with my aunt when I was just a kid, and I was fascinated by the pictures in the photograph album we looked at. Just before I left I took one last look at the albums, and on a sudden impulse I slipped out some of the pictures. I don't know what made me do it. It was the only time in my life I ever stole anything, and I felt terribly guilty for a long time afterwards. When I got home, I hid them so well it was years before I found them again."

"And it was discovered, your theft?"

"I never knew. There was a rift in the family, and I didn't see my aunt for several years. By that time, we had other things on our minds."

Again, an expectant silence, but this time Harriet volunteered no further information.

"What a funny character you are, Harriet," Hope said. "I'm glad we managed this lunch together. I hope we'll have lots more."

After Hope walked off up the street, Harriet went into the house, sat on her bed for a while, and then came out again and walked back in the direction of the theatre. She was headed towards the liquor store, intending to pick up a paper on the way so that she could look up places available for short-term rent.

V

Harriet always knew her real life began when she was twelve years old. She'd known at the time that something important had happened, but it wasn't until much later that she understood she'd started out then on the path she would tread as long as she lived.

Before she was twelve, Harriet had never had a proper holiday — the kind where you went to the beach and swam in the sea. She'd never even been off the prairies before. And then suddenly they let her go for two whole weeks to stay in a huge house by the ocean. It was almost like going to another country, because it was on an island off the west coast where there were whales and cougars and bears. And she went with her aunt Nina, who was the person she admired most in the world.

Even now, she couldn't figure out why her mother had allowed it. Perhaps it had to do with her mother's operation and her need for peace and quiet when she got out of hospital. But that wasn't the real explanation, because Harriet at twelve would have been a help rather than a burden. Perhaps her aunt had paid for something and done so on certain conditions. It was all part of the undercurrent of tension that riddled the relationship between her mother and her aunt.

Aunt Nina came out regularly every spring before they went out to the acreage for the summer. The whole time she was with them, the house was fraught with tension that mounted gradually and resulted in at least one big explosion. It was so uncomfortable that Harriet couldn't understand why her aunt kept putting up with it.

"Why do you hate her?" she asked her mother.

"I don't hate her," her mother said. "She's my sister, isn't she? She gets on my nerves is all, same as you and Donna." That seemed reasonable enough because Harriet and Donna fought all the time.

"Why does she keep coming out here?" she asked.

"Because we're family. The only one she's got."

Her mother said it with contempt, the same tone she always used for speaking of Aunt Nina. Harriet had been afraid her aunt would stomp out and they'd never see her again. But she never fought back, and Harriet often felt sorry for her, alone in the world and treated so badly by the only family she had. There was something pathetic about the way she hung about the house on sufferance, knowing she wasn't welcome.

On the other hand, it was hard to feel sorry for Aunt Nina for long because she was so elegant. She held herself erect and walked with such an air in her high-heeled shoes that people turned to stare at her. Even if she did live alone, she had plenty of money, wore beautiful clothes, and drove a big car. She was a private secretary to a rich man in British Columbia. Harriet wasn't sure of the details and didn't exactly know what a private secretary or a pulp mill was.

"Do you wish you looked like Aunt Nina?" Harriet once incautiously asked her mother.

"We could all look like that if we lived the way she does," her mother concluded when she finished blowing off a head of steam.

Her mother held it against her younger sister that she was single and worked for a living. That didn't seem fair, because it wasn't Aunt Nina's fault that her fiancé had been killed in a farm accident. One of the neighbours was a widow who lived alone and had a job, and Harriet's mother said she was very brave, but she never praised Aunt Nina. She just hinted that if Harriet spent too much time around her aunt some kind of contamination would rub off and she'd end up being an old maid and a career girl.

Anyway, it was a huge surprise when they told Harriet one night while they were having supper that her mother had to go into hospital and she was being sent to stay with her aunt. Donna didn't mind that she wasn't going too; she had a boyfriend and she didn't like being separated from him for a minute. Besides, they all knew Harriet was her aunt's favorite. That was another thing her mother held against Aunt Nina. She talked about favouritism as if it was one of the seven deadly sins, even though she favoured Donna in a hundred different ways.

The main thing Harriet worried about was travelling by herself on the train. A woman from church was going to a convention in Vancouver, and she promised to keep an eye on Harriet, but the woman was going to sleep in her seat on the train, while Aunt Nina had booked a sleeper for Harriet.

"There's only a curtain separating those sleepers from the corridor," her sister said. "What'll you do if you feel a hand creeping up your leg in the night?"

"I suppose she'll spoil you rotten," her mother said, "and nothing'll be good enough for you when you get home."

"A couple of weeks aren't going to change her," her father said.

In spite of all her fears, Harriet enjoyed the journey to the coast and slept well at night, lulled by the steady rhythm of the train. It seemed no time at all before they were in Vancouver. She had no problem spotting her aunt at the train station, because she stood out in the crowd, being so well dressed and wearing a perky hat on her head. She knew how to dress because she'd been to Paris once and picked up a lot of hints. She put dabs of rouge on her earlobes and had bottles of French perfume on her dressing table. She showed Harriet how to put just the right amount behind her own ears, and she let her try on her hats. Harriet even met her aunt's boss.

The day after she arrived there was a thump at the door, the sound of a key turning in the lock, and there he was. Aunt Nina looked astonished.

"I have my niece here," she said.

"Ah yes," he said. "It slipped my mind."

"Well you might as well come in now that you're here," her aunt said. "This is Harriet."

"I have an aunt called Harriet," he said.

"Everyone has an aunt called Harriet," her aunt said very tartly.

Harriet wondered how she could talk to her boss like that. She thought he was stupid, and she didn't appreciate comments on her name.

It was the first time Harriet had seen anybody rich and famous close up, and he was a big disappointment. He looked like any other middle-aged man, and she thought he was uglier than most, with not much hair and great bushy eyebrows. She changed her mind when they stood at the window and watched him stride down the street to his car. It was twice as big as any other car on the street, and a man in a uniform jumped out, ran around, and opened the door for him.

Harriet's father sometimes drove a cab in winter, but he didn't wear a uniform and jump out to open doors for people. It was dangerous work because he never knew who'd jump in the back seat or what state they'd be in.

Mr. Herbert seemed even less ordinary when she saw the house on the beach he was letting them have all to themselves. They went by ferry to Vancouver Island, took another small ferry when they got there, and then drove up the coast a short distance to the house. It was a huge place, and it wasn't even his main house, just his summer home. There was glass all along the front so they could look out at the sea, and it was surrounded by little cottages. There were two guest houses, two cottages for the help, and a kind of greenhouse with an indoor swimming pool inside it.

At first it felt to Harriet like going into one of her friend's houses and raiding the fridge when their parents were out of town. She thought her aunt felt the same way, because she tiptoed around looking at everything as if she'd never seen it before. She said that she'd once stayed for a whole winter in the gardener's cottage when she was working on a project for her boss.

There were photographs in silver frames on the tables. One was of the queen, not in evening dress like the one on the wall of the principal's office at school, but in summer clothes in the garden of this very house. There was a photograph of Mr. Herbert on his yacht with a huge fish he'd caught, and there were a lot of photographs of his wife and two sons. In the pictures Mrs. Herbert was always sitting down or lying in a deck chair, and Aunt Nina said she was ill with MS. In one photo she was in evening dress in a wheelchair. Her aunt said that was all right because Roger didn't care for dancing. He said, "Why dance when you can hire someone to do it for you?"

"But someone can't dance *for* you," Harriet said.

"He's just kidding," her aunt said.

There was one photograph of a tall woman holding a dog on the lawn in front of a big ivy-covered house.

"Who's that?" Harriet asked, pointing to it, and it seemed to take her aunt a while to work out who she was.

"That's Mazo," she said, eventually. It was the first time Harriet heard the name, and she looked up, her attention caught by something her aunt's voice as she spoke it.

"Who's Mazo?" she asked.

"She's his cousin," her aunt said. "She's a famous writer. Mazo de la Roche."

"Is she a foreigner?" Harriet asked.

"No, she's as Canadian as you and me," said her aunt, "but she gave herself a French name. Her real name's Maisie Roach, but woe betide anybody who calls her by her real name. Roger tried it once and she nearly bit his head off."

"Why did she change her name?"

"I guess she thought more people would buy her books if they saw a fancy name on the cover."

"And did they?"

"Did they what?"

"Did more people buy the books because of the name?"

"I don't know if that was why, but plenty of people bought them. Buy them."

"Have you read them?"

"Oh yes," her aunt said, "I get every one the minute it comes out."

"What are they about?" Harriet said.

"About a family called the Whiteoaks who live in a big house called Jalna."

The first day when they came in from walking on the beach, the housekeeper, who lived in one of the cottages, came to ask about their dinner. Did they want her to serve it? She said she'd made a cold meal because of the hot weather. She hoped that would be all right. Aunt Nina said that would be fine and to just set it out and they'd look after themselves. After she left, they explored the kitchen, still feeling like intruders. There was lobster salad in a glass bowl. Her aunt flicked the bowl with her middle finger and thumb and it chimed like a bell. She said that was how you could tell real crystal. The dining room table was set with silver that gleamed and dishes with gold rims. They lit all six candles in the candlesticks. "Why not?" her aunt said.

Then she pulled a bottle of champagne out of the fridge. She'd never opened a bottle of bubbly herself before, but she was willing to give it a try. She told Harriet to look out because you could lose an eye when the cork flew out. After a lot of squeezing, it flew out with a loud bang and a lot of foam went on the floor.

"This stuff costs about what your dad makes in one week," her aunt said. She gave Harriet a glass of it on condition she didn't tell her mother. It prickled the lining of her nose and made her burp like a frog. Her aunt finished most of it, as it seemed a pity to let it go to waste and by the next day it would be flat.

The weather held for the first week, and then it started to rain. Harriet didn't really mind, because the house was more fun than the beach. She could sit by the window and watch the deer come out of the trees at the edge of the lawn. She'd never seen them close up before. They were really beautiful with long, thin legs that looked as if they'd snap easily like the long stems on the wine glasses they used. The housekeeper came in and lit a fire, and her aunt found a stack of photograph albums in a closet and they sat side by side on the sofa looking at them.

Aunt Nina didn't mind Harriet asking questions about Roger and his wife. If she didn't want to answer she said, "That's for me to know and you to find out." She knew all about them because she was like one of the family, so Harriet thought her aunt did have a family after all. She was so close to his wife and sons that when they travelled she made all the arrangements. She even did their Christmas shopping.

When she asked about Mrs. Herbert, Aunt Nina said, "Oh, she's a sweet lady. She never complains, and she's so grateful for everything you do. She can't thank you enough." It was while they were looking at the albums that Harriet started putting two and two together. Actually it was her friend Fiona who had first planted the idea in her head weeks ago. Fiona was always talking about whether it was better to marry for money or love. Harriet said she wasn't sure she wanted to get married at all, and she told Fiona about her aunt.

"She's probably his mistress," Fiona said.

"No, she isn't," Harriet said. "She's too prim and proper."

Fiona knew a lot more than Harriet because she came from a broken home. She didn't call it that, she just said her mum and dad were divorced. Her dad wanted her to go and live with him in England where he said she'd have a better life and go to a good school. Fiona said he really wanted her just to spite her mum.

"They're having a custody battle over me," Fiona told her proudly.

64 | Joan Givner

"Custardy?" Harriet said.

She thought that if her aunt was Mr. Herbert's mistress, she and his wife should be bitter enemies, but she gradually saw that the person her aunt really hated was the writer. There were lots of pictures of her with Caroline, her secretary-companion, and her beautiful daughter, Antoinette.

"Why are there no pictures of Mazo's husband?" Harriet asked.

"She hasn't got a husband."

"Like you," Harriet said.

"No," her aunt said, "not like me. She doesn't want anything to do with men. At least not in that way."

"Well, how did she get the daughter?" Harriet asked.

"You tell me," her aunt said. "Then we'll both know."

The dinners were the best part of the day. Every night there was a surprise. Harriet couldn't believe all the different dishes the housekeeper made. When it was cold, she made hot meals and left them in the oven with the timer on. Sometimes there were things Harriet didn't recognize, and they turned out to be pheasant and venison. At first Harriet said it made her feel funny eating deer when they were so beautiful, but her aunt pointed out that she didn't mind eating chicken and lamb and they were pretty cute too. Harriet agreed that if you thought too much about it, you'd end up not eating anything.

She began to look forward to her glass of wine each night. Her aunt drank the rest of the bottle and then started to talk in a different way, quietly and confidingly. With the next glass she became sad and sometimes started to cry. When she got very upset, she didn't have coffee but had a glass of brandy instead.

It always turned out the same. First she complained she'd never marry and have a family like everyone else. Then she started blaming people. Those rich folk can do what they fucking want. Want a car, buy one. Want a mansion, buy one. Want a lover, buy one. Want a baby, buy one.

"But you can't buy a baby," Harriet said.

"That's what you think," her aunt said. "There's nothing in this world that doesn't have a price tag on it. That's what Roger says."

"Who could you buy a baby from?"

"From some damn fool who has no money, no family, and not enough sense to know what she's doing. That's why I want you to make something of your life and get an education, so nobody can push you around."

The next day Aunt Nina seemed to have forgotten what they had talked about the night before. They had breakfast in a room called the solarium, and her aunt took Aspirin and said she shouldn't have finished off all the wine.

It got so that if Harriet was curious about something during the day, she saved it up and asked her aunt when she was on her third glass of wine.

"Your fiancé that was killed...?" she said.

"Oh, him. He was nothing," her aunt said. "He was a pig farmer, for God's sake."

"How did you meet Mr. Herbert?" she said.

"Applied for the job and we hit it off from the word go."

"Why would the cousin want a kid?" Harriet said.

"I wondered that myself," her aunt said. "I asked Roger one time."

"What did he say?" Harriet said.

"He said, 'Don't ask me, I've never been able to figure out why women want most of the things they want.'"

Harriet sat very still, waiting for what would come next.

"I thought at first she wanted to raise a girl to break somebody's heart. You see, she only wanted a girl. That was the condition. It had to be a girl or the arrangement was off. She would-
n't take a boy."

Harriet sat so still she was hardly breathing.

"Then when I read the books," her aunt went on, "I finally solved the puzzle. What does she know about how ordinary
people live and raise kids? She lives with Caroline, just the two
of them, in that mansion with her chauffeur and her gardener
and her cook and all her money. She needed a kid to give her
a window on ordinary life. She wanted to watch her grow up,
like somebody in a lab watching a guinea pig. She wanted to
write about her in those books. There's more ways than one of
using people. One way or another they live off you and suck
your blood...."

"Is Antoinette happy?"

"Well, look at those pictures. You've seen her in her riding
habit with her pony taking part in horse shows, and in her
fancy costumes for parties, dressed up like a little doll. What do
you think?"

"Suppose Antoinette wanted to run away and go back to
her own mother?"

"How could she when she doesn't even know who her
mother is or where she came from?"

Then her aunt put her head down on the table and cried.
Harriet was ashamed of being so nosy, but she couldn't seem to
stop herself. She couldn't find out enough about the mysterious
girl in the pictures, who was so rich but didn't know where she
came from or who she was.

"If you're so interested in Antoinette," her aunt said, "you
can read about her in the books."

Harriet didn't understand, so her aunt went over to the bookshelf, picked up one of the books, opened it, and started reading:

> Adeline appeared from the stable riding Wakefield's old pony. It was a dark bay with a small neat head and kind eyes. She pressed her knees against it, her lips pouted in pride.
>
> "Look at her!" exclaimed Piers. "Look at her feet and her legs! Just right, by gosh! Look at her hands and her wrist! Adeline, round your wrists just a *bit* more! *She's* going to make a good one." He grinned triumphantly at Renny. "*She* won't be tossed off like a feather pillow!"
>
> "I want to jump!" cried Adeline. She headed her pony for straight at one of the gates.

Then Harriet began to see that although it was a story, the writer had stuck a real person in it. When she described a young girl called Adeline, who was the daughter of the master of Jalna, she was really describing Antoinette, the girl in the photograph.

When Harriet first saw a movie she thought the people on the screen were real people, and she was shocked to learn they only acting, like she and her friends did when they played "let's pretend." It had seemed like a kind of betrayal, after she'd been so caught up in their lives. Later, she laughed at her younger self for being so easily taken in. But now she was learning that books work in the opposite way. When you read them you thought the characters were all made up by the author, but they were sometimes real people the author knew and put into the book with their names changed. It was all very confusing.

She could see that Adeline in the book looked exactly like Antoinette in the picture; they both had long, dark hair drawn behind their ears in exactly the same way, with tendrils that escaped and gave them both a wild gypsy look. But when she asked her aunt if Antoinette was "strong-willed" and "arrogant," her aunt said they had no way of knowing. Perhaps Mazo had just made that up. Not knowing exactly where Adeline ended and Antoinette began made the book even more interesting to Harriet. Once she started reading it she didn't want to put it down, and she read it from cover to cover.

When they left the island she didn't want to leave the book behind, but her aunt said she had the complete set back in her apartment. And before she took Harriet back to the train, she let her choose one of the books for a parting gift. Harriet stood in front of the bookcase for a long time trying to decide which one she wanted to read next. Her aunt said she didn't have to worry, because every public library, no matter how small it was, was sure to have all of Mazo's books.

They asked her a lot of questions when she got back.

"Did you meet the boyfriend?" her sister said.

"What boyfriend?" Harriet said.

"You haven't said very much about all the great things you saw," her mother said. "Was it not as grand as you expected?"

"It was fine," Harriet said.

She'd decided even before she went that she wasn't going to say a word about her aunt's place and the holiday if her mother started quizzing her.

"She'll tell you when she's good and ready," her dad said, looking over the top of the paper. "Give her time to settle back down after all the excitement."

He smiled at Harriet, and she smiled back at him. Her aunt wasn't the only person who stood up for her.

Harriet never did say anything about her holiday, because soon it was the harvest season and they were too busy baling hay to think about her. So it all got buried inside her head. But from that time on, she was a reader, going regularly to the library, working her way through the whole Jalna series, and then starting at the beginning again.

VI

FOR RENT: Top floor of house in quiet neighbourhood. Suite of rooms + attic. View of lake and legislative building. 584-3851

The advertisement was conspicuous among the other rental property ads for its lack of factual information about rent, date of occupancy, and whether furnished or unfurnished. But the suggestion of an attic, a quiet neighbourhood, and a view was enough to send Harriet downstairs to the telephone in the hall.

"Lilian Posey speaking."

"I'm calling about the ad in the paper."

"Of course you are."

"Is it furnished or unfurnished?"

"Well, you won't have to sleep on the floor. There's some furniture, certainly, but I can't vouch for its condition. It's been a number of years since I've been up there myself. You have to realize that I can no longer manage the stairs. Even a few stairs are very difficult for me."

It sounded more promising all the time. Spacious, on the second floor of a house, and with an elderly guardian below, incapable of climbing the stairs.

"The ad doesn't mention the rent."

"That's true." Nothing more was forthcoming.

There was a long pause, after which Harriet asked if she might inspect the place and was invited to come over immediately.

"Do you take sugar in your tea?"

"No, I don't," said Harriet, who wasn't very keen on tea in the first place.

"That's just as well because I seem to have run out." This was said so sadly that Harriet immediately asked if she might bring some over.

"What kind would it be?" the voice asked eagerly.

"What would you prefer?"

"That depends on what's available."

"I suppose there's brown and white sugar, or cubes...."

"A little of each, please."

And so Harriet, carrying a brown paper bag containing four small packages with different kinds of sugar, set off across the park without needing to ask for directions towards Fortescue Street. That name, with the accent on the middle syllable, had come back to her with a long string of associations.

Harriet, seven or eight years old, was reading aloud in class from a book with large print and coloured pictures. She was a good reader with a strong carrying voice. But her performance had not been flawless. She'd stumbled over an unfamilar word. The word was "picturesque" — and she'd pronounced it "pictures-queue." The teacher had corrected her gently. It didn't rhyme with "Fortescue," she said, it rhymed with "desk." Thus the two words had been linked in her mind, each one reinforcing the meaning of the other.

Fortescue Street *was* picturesque. It was not one of the best streets, where rich people lived in mansions suggestive of ill-gotten gain and ostentation, but it was a good street, with substantial, unpretentious houses. Coming as she did from the grid of mean streets on the edge of town, Harriet had always walked down Fortescue Street with awe. It had seemed to her a reasonable goal to aspire to — living in a house on Fortescue Street. Her teacher, she learned later, lived on it herself, and no doubt that was why it sprang to her mind as an example of the wrong pronunciation of "picturesque." Perhaps she was proud of living there. But that was back then.

Now it was in a state of transition, because the young professionals preferred the new subdivisions that were encroaching like fungoid growths on the surrounding prairie. Even the city's former fringe of small frame houses and onion-domed churches was giving way to new houses; they were still flimsily built, but pretentious now and fronted with huge garages, as if the occupants were perpetually in motion and used the living quarters for brief pit stops before leaping into their cars and taking off again.

From Fortescue Street it was still possible to reach the park, the grocery store, and the centre of town on foot. Perhaps for that reason the relative scale and position of the houses and garages indicated saner priorities. The garages remained discreetly concealed behind the houses; their doors opened onto alleys through which drivers entered, leaving their cars and walking up flower-bordered paths to the back doors of their houses.

In front there were sidewalks broad enough to accommodate skipping rope jumpers and hopscotch players, evening strollers, young mothers with baby buggies, and — during the languor of hot summer afternoons — purveyors of Kool-Aid and cookies. And all this teeming life was shaded and protected by an arch of long-established Dutch elms. You could stand at one end of the street and look down a leafy tunnel. It was now a mixed enclave of old-timers, transient renters, and university professors with casual housekeeping and gardening arrangements. Yet there was a sense of life — organic, wholesome, struggling, and multigenerational.

When Harriet arrived at 2638, the door was slightly ajar and the voice she had heard on the telephone summoned her inside. A grey-haired woman, not nearly as old as she'd expected, was sitting in an armchair by the fireplace. One of the doors of the adjoining room was open, and through it Harriet caught a glimpse of a large abstract painting of a circle that was hung on the wall above the head of a double bed.

On the table beside Lilian was an electrical gadget for making tea and six cups and saucers, some of which had already been used. Harriet wondered if she had been preceded by other contenders for the attic, the quiet neighbourhood, and the view of the lake. The china was very good but chipped, the silver was Georgian and highly polished, and there was a small pair of tongs in anticipation of the sugar cubes.

"My goodness, what an expense," Lilian said when Harriet handed over the sugar, "but we can deduct it from the rent."

"Yes, I was wondering about that," Harriet said.

"Well, don't. It will be nominal. The situation is that my nephew likes me to have someone here in case I die in the night and no one finds me for several days."

She pressed a button and the gadget delivered tea into first one cup and then the other. Harriet saw that her knuckles were gnarled and swollen, probably from arthritis. But with great care and using both hands, she managed to deploy the tongs, putting three sugar cubes into her cup and wavering over a fourth. Either because it was too much effort or because she'd concluded the tea was sweet enough, she decided against the fourth cube.

"I rarely leave the house except for my doctors' appointments. My nephew likes me to have someone here as double security. Mrs. Pike comes in three days a week except when there are emergencies with the other clients whom she obliges or when she goes to a funeral. Mrs. Pike attends many funerals. They constitute her social life, and, fortunately for her, there seems to be a high mortality rate among her friends and acquaintances. But there's no need for you to be alarmed on my account, because I have no intention of dying before the next election."

Lilian was speaking as if Harriet's tenancy of the apartment was a foregone conclusion. It was an eerie repetition of the situation at the theatre when Harriet had learned that she had all along been chosen to play Mazo; the similarity made her think wildly for a moment that there was some great conspiracy afoot to trap her, and that she should flee this house and this town while there was still time.

"Do you take an interest in politics?" Lilian asked.

"Not very much, I'm afraid," said Harriet. "A little."

"Well, you'll have every opportunity to do so while you're here because I'll pass along the newspapers. And the crucial articles will be marked."

"Thank you," said Harriet.

"You can thank me best," said Lilian, "by disposing of them. This will be relatively easy. For you, that is, not for me."

"It will?" said Harriet.

"Yes, we're lucky enough to have a dumpster in the alley just by the side of our back gate."

"A dumpster?"

"A container for the garbage. You can put in newspapers and anything you wish. Old shoes, bottles … a wonderful thing, a dumpster. My nephew paints them."

"He decorates the dumpsters?"

"No, no. He's an artist and he specializes in alleyscapes with dumpsters. You'll see."

Harriet did see when she eventually made her way upstairs to inspect the rooms. The second floor had a sitting room at the front, overlooking the street. There was also a room with a daybed and a desk on which sat a television set. At the back there was a dining room with a small galley kitchen, and beside that a windowless bathroom with avocado green fixtures. Another portable television set sat on the kitchen counter. A narrow flight of stairs led up to a third floor.

The attic was wonderful. It ran the length of the house and was big enough to serve as a small theatre, except that a large double bed stood on the raised dais where the stage might have been. The walls sloped sharply, but there were skylights set into them and windows at each end so that the room was very bright. From the window at the back of the house Harriet could see the dome of the legislative building and the view of the lake mentioned in the advertisement. In the narrow space between the sloping walls and the floor there were paintings, two on each side, of back alleys with dumpsters, done at different times of the year to depict the theme of the four seasons. There were no curtains in the windows, and the late afternoon sunlight slanted over the paintings in a curious imitation of the patterns of light in the pictures themselves.

"I love it, especially the attic," said Harriet when she returned downstairs.

"Then I think we shall suit each other perfectly," said Lilian. It occurred to Harriet that she should say something about herself.

"I'm an actor, here for the next play at The Globe." For a moment she thought that her occupation and short tenure might disqualify her as a tenant.

"I knew that as soon as I heard your voice," Lilian said. "You must have good breath control. I might call for your help occasionally in reading things and blowing up balloons. I get out of puff very quickly myself."

"Balloons?" said Harriet. "You mean for a party?"

"No. They are for another purpose entirely which I shall explain later. I might also ask you to water my plants, because Mrs. Pike tries to kill them off. They are cacti and succulents and pretty hardy. In fact, it's often assumed they don't need any water at all. That's a great mistake. They do need water from time to time, as well as direct sun."

Harriet had noticed that the sun room along the end of the room was filled with plants. She could see how the housekeeper might resent looking after them, because they were rather ugly, spiky plants.

"I think you'll find everything you need upstairs. Mrs. Pike has made up the bed and she'll clean up for you, if you wish."

"Oh no," said Harriet hastily, "I wouldn't like that."

"I don't blame you," said Lilian. "I don't like it either, but I'm in no position to resist. And I should warn you, there's no television set, and I don't allow television in the house."

"Well, it won't be a problem," Harriet said. She was addicted to watching the Weather Network, but it seemed a small price to pay for all the benefits of living with Lilian. She wondered momentarily about the sets she had seen upstairs, but assumed they no longer functioned.

"One thing I do intend to hold onto is my mind."

"Your mind?" Harriet said, not getting the connection.

"They've done studies, you know, on people's brains. They wired them up and found that there's less activity when they watch television than at any other time, even when they're fast asleep. Television induces a comatose state in the viewer. I think that explains a lot about the spread of Alzheimer's disease, don't you?"

Harriet allowed that it might.

"There's a lot of nonsense talked about failing memory in the elderly — senior moments and so on. It isn't memory that goes, it's the power of concentration, and that's entirely different. As you get older, nothing you do has the urgency or importance it had before, and so it's difficult to summon up the effort to concentrate. That's only one part of it. To concentrate you need to clear a great deal of space and eliminate distractions."

Harriet waited to hear more.

"There are altogether too many electronic devices. People do too many things at the same time — reading and listening to music, watching television and doing needlework, cooking and listening to the news on the radio. In the morning I see the neighbours scurrying down the street to work, all of them wearing tennis shoes and earphones, their heads wired for sound. It's terrifying to think of it. Concentration gets so fragmented that people lose contact with their own thoughts and then lose the knack of thinking altogether. Superficiality reigns."

"'We live, I regret to say, in an age of surfaces,'" quoted Harriet, automatically.

"I was not altogether truthful, Harriet, when I told my nephew to state in the advertisement that this is a quiet neighbourhood. The neighbours on either side have electronic security systems. If burglars try to break and enter during their absence, a siren goes off that disturbs the entire neighbourhood. Unfortunately, the things often go off spontaneously and shatter the peace when there's no burglar in sight. It's so unnecessary. I have my own perfectly good security system."

"I suppose you're less likely to have burglars if you're always home," Harriet said.

"Well, you suppose wrongly," said Lilian. "Burglars these days are undeterred by the occupants of houses, especially during the night. It's for this purpose that I use the balloons. I place several beside my bed. I'm a light sleeper, and if I hear a noise during the night, I take a pin and pop them — one, two, three, four. They sound exactly like gunshots."

Harriet thought they probably sounded exactly like balloons popping. She hoped that blowing up a lot of balloons would not be a nightly ritual.

"It's one of my safeguards," Lilian said. "I have others, which eventually I shall explain to you."

Lilian required no signature on a contract and no deposit, and it was agreed that Harriet should move in as soon as she wished, probably the next afternoon.

"Before you leave," Lilian said, "could I ask you to clip these two things out of the paper. My hands are unusually stiff and awkward today."

"Are they people you know?" asked Harriet, seeing that the items were from the obituary section.

"Not at all," said Lilian, "but they are very singular and significant and they connect. It's important to find connections."

Harriet, glancing at them, couldn't immediately see the connection:

GREGORY, Mary Dorota — this gracious lady answered when Christ came knocking at the door on August 6th at the age of eighty-six years. She is survived by her son, Michael of Saskatoon. She is predeceased by her husband, Myroslaw (1980), her father, Vladimir (1930), and her mother, Olga (1975). She is resting at Flemings Funeral Home on Thursday 7-9 p.m. with the reciting of the Rosary at 7:30 p.m. and Friday from 2-5 and 7-9 p.m. with Panakhyda at 7:30 p.m. Her son will receive family and friends on Saturday, September 5th at 10:30 a.m. until the start of Divine Liturgy at 11:00 a.m. in St. Ignacius Ukrainian Catholic Church. Interment to follow at Heavenly Rest Cemetery. As your expression of sympathy, donations may be made to the Order of the Sisters Servants of Mary Immaculate.

CRAWFORD, Erica Margaret — suddenly at the age of eighty-six while on a swimming expedition with friends at Waskesiew. Asked that morning if she was well enough to join the outing, Ricki replied that she would go swimming if it killed her. She died doing what she loved best. As a young girl in Halifax, N.S., she sang and danced in local theatre productions and, at 16, played piano for the silent pictures features at the Gaiety. She became a registered nurse in 1931, graduating from Hartford Hospital in Connecticut. While in Hartford she

became a charter member of the Mark Twain
Masquers Little Theater troupe. She returned to
Halifax when war was declared. Ricki moved
to Melford ten years ago. She will be greatly
missed by her loving daughter, Frances
(Michael), and grandchildren Sarah, Rowena,
and Jason. A celebration of Ricki's life will be
held at the Melton Little Theater at 7:00 p.m.
September 15ᵗʰ. Remembrances may be made
to the C.N.I.B.

"Do you see the connection?" Lilian said.

"They're both eighty-six," Harriet said.

"They *are* both eighty-six, and you'd think at that age they'd
have learned some sense. Instead of which, they both had exag-
gerated notions of their own importance. And they were both
out of contact with reality. Isn't that absurd? 'She died doing
what she loved best.'"

"She did, though, didn't she?" said Harriet.

"Lots of people die doing what they love best," said Lilian.
"Drug addicts who overdose on heroin, bank robbers who get
shot in their line of work, greedy people who choke on steak
bones, drinkers who down bottles of brandy and vodka that finish them off. They all die doing what they love best, but it would
be ridiculous to remark on it in their obituary notices."

"But Erica was more admirable than foolish, wasn't she?"
Harriet said. "She loved swimming and she knew it was risky at
her age, but she refused to submit to the limitations of old age."

"You take a very sympathetic view of it, Harriet, but I see it
differently. I don't think for a minute she meant it literally when
she said she would swim if it killed her. She was speaking

thoughtlessly and boastfully. She would have preferred to live on, even if it meant giving up swimming. Swimming isn't something to die for. She was a self-centred old woman and she probably looked a fright in a bathing costume. And then think of the trouble — fishing her out of the sea, trying to revive her, running for help. Not to mention the guilt she inflicted on those who permitted her to swim."

Did Lilian always have to have the last word, Harriet wondered as she walked back across the park, feeling very pleased with the transaction. She loved the suite of rooms, but she'd also developed a strong affinity for Lilian, in spite or perhaps because of her eccentricities. She was no fool, just an old woman, immobilized by illness, rendered dependent, prey to intruders of all kinds. Yet, she'd created a space around herself and she defended it. One last touch had made Harriet feel more like a co-conspirator than a tenant. Just as she was leaving, Lilian had called her back.

"One more thing, Harriet. We have to hide the sugar. I'm not allowed to have it."

"Good God," said Harriet. "Are you diabetic?"

"Hand me the grey cushion from there," Lilian said, ignoring the question. She proceeded to unzip the covering and stow the sugar inside the cushion, directing Harriet to replace it with the cushion from her chair.

"I think I'm old enough, don't you, Harriet, to take risks if I wish and to calculate the results without being placed under surveillance?"

And die doing what you love best? Harriet was tempted to say. She thought that Lilian, confined within four walls and addicted to a forbidden substance, must have recognized in her a natural kinship. They were ideal co-conspirators against some vague, nameless authority licensed to oppress them. They shared the same fears, she thought, remembering Lilian's peroration on the subject of memory loss and failing mental powers. She was sure Hope had no such fears; her mind worked so effectively that you could almost hear its mechanism ticking over as she talked.

Harriet felt smugly that she'd outsmarted Hope by staking out her own territory in the town. She'd been back in this place for such a short time and already she had found a home and established some complicated relationships — intrusive and unsettling, to be sure, but perhaps that was inevitable in a small town.

VII

It was the start of summer school, and a holiday camp atmosphere prevailed on the campus. Harriet walked along the familiar paths towards the audio-visual department under the hot noonday sun. There had been two film versions of Mazo's novels — a Hollywood movie in 1953 and a CBC television production in 1972. In order to build up the background to the play, they were to spend the next few days in a screening room watching the television version. Harriet liked to arrive early and wait, leaning against the wall, outside the door for a class to emerge blinking like owls from a showing of *Oedipus Rex* or *The Glass Menagerie*. She usually walked alone, but often she heard footsteps pursuing her and was hailed and then accompanied by Hope or the director, or both.

The director, Sandy, was from Santa Fe, a visiting professor in the theatre department and a close friend of Hope's, though Harriet sensed tension between them and wondered if it augured future conflicts.

"Lak fleas on a dog's ear," Sandy said one afternoon, joining her, gesturing towards the mass of students who lay about the grass reading, picnicking, and sleeping. Hope's teaching duties had kept her in the classroom, so Harriet was free to enjoy Sandy's quirky observations about the play and their surroundings.

At first Harriet had trouble placing Sandy and had thought that the dark skin and jet black hair might indicate Aztec or Indian blood, but Hope had laughed and said it was nothing so exotic. Sandy was Jewish and had arrived in Santa Fe by way of Brooklyn and Chicago. They had met at a conference in Texas. Sandy soon afterwards had confirmed Hope's account with a soulful rendering of "When it's Rosh Hashanah time in Dixieland."

"Did you ever live in Dixieland?" said Harriet.

"Dixieland!" said Sandy, mocking her pronunciation. "You make it sound like Disneyland. You probably have it confused with Disneyland. You Canadians and your ignorance of your southern neighbours! You think the four major cities in the U.S. are Disneyland, Hollywood, and Las Vegas. Everyone I run into here has made a pilgrimage to one of those places."

"That's three," said Harriet. "What's the fourth?"

"The fourth's Graceland, because you all love Elvis. You haven't a geographical clue. Admit, Harriet, you couldn't find New Mexico on the map if I gave you a hundred dollars!"

"And you couldn't find the Gaspé Peninsula or Newfoundland or the Queen Charlottes," said Hope, who had materialized beside them. "You get very tiresome on this subject, Sandy."

"Thought you were in class," Sandy said.

"First few days of classes they don't have any books. I let them out early," Hope said. "Have you thought some more about the soundtrack of the TV scenes?"

They engaged constantly in verbal skirmishes, and Sandy usually won. The only subject on which they were in agreement was their contempt for the theatre's artistic director, Beth Grissley, and her constituency of season ticket holders. Just now their chief topic of disagreement was Sandy's inspiration that they project scenes from the television series onto a screen behind Mazo and Caroline when they were acting out their private play. Hope granted that it was an interesting idea and liked the way it emphasized the connection between the private play and the Whiteoaks Saga. But she had reservations about its being a distraction, and she definitely objected to Sandy's using the television soundtrack as a muted background murmur.

The projector seemed to be a key part of Sandy's technical repertoire. For the read-through, the actors sat around a table without their personal copies of the script and read from a script projected page by page onto a screen at the end of the room. Harriet felt stripped and exposed without props and a wad of paper to shield her. And because she was short-sighted, it was like having her eyes tested or doing a basic reading exercise in elementary school.

Sandy made no attempt to accommodate her disability but merely encouraged her to take her time, read slowly, and breathe, and so the whole process went along haltingly:

> CARO: I thought you were from the *Boston Globe!*
>
> REPORTER: Not the *Boston Globe. The Toronto Globe.* You'll be able to see the write-up in Saturday's edition.

CARO: *The Toronto Globe.* Well, I'll be...

(She bundles him out the door and calls out to the back of the apartment.)

Mazo, you can come out now.

MAZO: Caroline ... what have you ... done? You gave ... him ... the Presid ... sorry ... the Prime Minister ... Minister's bouquet ...

DIRECTOR: OK, Harriet. No problem. Just take it slowly. Take your own time. And *breathe.* Brandi!

CARO: Oh, sorry. Well, I think I removed the card. And, in any case, one bunch of hothouse flowers is exactly like another.

DIRECTOR: Harriet!

MAZO: Oh, yes, sorry! But, Caroline, the things you ... you ... told him —

CARO: Don't worry. Everything was quite consistent with what I told the reporter from the Ottawa paper yesterday.

MAZO: It's not the ... constancy ... consistency ... I'm worried about, it's the truth.

(Picking up a newspaper and reading) "Of noble ... French ... origin." Have you ... forgotten ... all ... the ... Roach graves ... in the cemetery ... in New ... Newmarket ... where I just ... happen ... happened ... to be born?

DIRECTOR: Good, Harriet. Just relax, and breathe. Take it slowly. Brandi!

CARO: Don't be absurd, Mazo! No one's going to go to Newmarket and check headstones on graves. I said you were born in Toronto.

MAZO: You said one of my ... ancestors ... was ... *guillotined*.

CARO: You always talk about your uncle Frank who was killed on your seventh birthday.

MAZO: But he was ... wasn't in the ... French Revolution ... and he was ... wasn't guillotined. He was killed in an ... industry ... industrial ... accident at the cane factory in Newmarket.

CARO: And how did he die?

MAZO: He was decaff ... decapitated.

CARO: Well, there you are! He was decaf-
        feinated ... fuck. (general laughter) Oh
        Christ! He was decapitated. That's
        exactly the same as being guillotined.
        It's just another way of saying it!

MAZO: It's not literal ... literally the same.
        There's a slight time ... difference of
        several hundred years. And the name's ...
        Hugue ... not, not ... Huge Knot ...
        How *do* you pronounce it anyway?

DIRECTOR: Hugh-ge-no. OK, I get the message,
        Brandi. Let's break for coffee. It's going
        well, but we'll scrap that Huguenot/
        Huge Knot bit. It's just Hope's attempt
        at humour.

Harriet looked around anxiously, but Hope must have slipped out at some point. At the break, instead of leaving the room, they brought their coffee back to the table, and Sandy held forth about the method, how it reinforced the communal nature of their project, like eating from a common bowl, and how the slower pace allowed time for the imagination to connect with the text, let the lines sink in, and eased them over the process of getting ready to act. Also reading from a distance required a physical effort, so the whole body was engaged.

"All that shit about connecting with the text. I think we're being fucking guinea pigs," said Brandi when they were in the bathroom together. "It's a load of bull. Right?"

"It's given me a blinding headache," said Harriet.

All the same, when they resumed the reading, Sandy's explanation seemed to make sense. Reading from a common script was curiously hypnotic; eventually they fell into a shared rhythm, bouncing their lines off each other, Harriet's long pauses between phrases being picked up by Brandi.

CARO: But what can I say? That we grew up in small rented houses, all jammed up together to save money? That we got hardly any education? That I work in an office to support us in this rooming house? That you changed your name from Roach because you were ashamed of it? How can one explain to reporters?

MAZO: I don't know ... I don't know ... anything any more. I feel exactly as if I had ... been. De-capitated.

CARO: Don't you always say that we can ... change our lives ... if only we let our imaginations soar?

MAZO: Caroline, yours soars at the ... wrong time and in the ... wrong places. It's alright to invent things when we do ... the play and when we talk ... to each other. Newspapermen and ... reporters are different. I believe ... they ... check up on things. They might ask people about us. Mrs.

Pringle, for example. She knows we don't have an ... ancestor ... ancestral ... home.

CARO: Let's never talk to reporters again. Let's just live quietly so that we can be who we want to be. So that we can imagine anything and no one will reproach us or laugh at us or expose us.

MAZO: I think we were ... happier before all this ... excitement happened. Before I won the prize. I hate ... publicity. I hate everything it brings. I hate the phone calls. I dread the doorbell. Ringing. I loathe the ... bouquets. They make me sneeze. I'm glad you gave the ... Prime Minister's flowers away.

CARO: They were horrible hothouse flowers, anyway. (They are laughing somewhat hysterically when they hear a tapping at the door.)

MRS. P: My dears, there's a reporter from the *New York Times* on the telephone. Will you come at once?

MAZO: No, I won't. You'll have to tell him, Mrs. Pringle, that there will be no more interviews.

CARO: Miss de la Roche is avoiding publicity from now on.

MAZO: It interferes. Too much. With her writing.

CARO: Henceforth, her hobby is privacy!

MAZO: And tell the man from the *Times*, Mrs. Pringle ..., we are leaving for our ancestral home. In England.

(Mrs. Pringle leaves.)

CARO: But, Mazo. What did you say? You were scolding me a moment ago for saying we had an ancestral home.

MAZO: True. But, Caroline, while I was listening to you describe the place we have ... don't have ... I thought what a wonderful idea it was. It's exactly what we need. Why don't we ... acquire ... one immediately?

CARO: We can certainly afford it.

MAZO: There are such places. We could find one easily.

CARO: We could sail across the Atlantic as soon as we've packed.

MAZO: And stay there for the rest of our lives.

CARO: And never come back to this benighted
          city. And I can leave my job.

MAZO: And I can write the next book. It will go
          very quickly, Caroline, with you there to do
          the play.

CARO: The play. Do you realize we haven't done
          our play for days?

MAZO: That's why I feel decapitated. When I'm cut
          off from the play I feel like a walking ghost.

(The Jalna music starts softly.)

CARO: Renny ... this house ... this Jalna ... I have
          the strangest feeling about it. I think that
          it's a living being instead of a house. I feel
          its pulse, its heartbeat. I imagine it listening
          to us all the time. On dark nights when the
          wind blows off the lake and the ivy flaps
          against the windowpanes I wake suddenly
          as if someone had called my name: Alayne
          (the name echoes Alayne, Alayne, Alayne).
          Even when I'm walking alone in the ravine
          I hear murmurs as if the trees were alive
          and watching me and whispering.

MAZO: All these people tangled together like badly
          cast fishing lines. Too many people have been
          born here, have laughed and been angry and

outrageous with each other. Too many people have died already. There are too many ...
ancestral ... bones propped up against the
mantel shelf. And yet, I'm part of it. I could-
n't escape if I wanted to ... I don't even want
to any more. I have no life other than this....
What is this place called Jalna anyway? What
am I? And what are you? Why are we all
here, all these warm-blooded hungry people,
in this house called Jalna? (The word echoes
and fades, Jalna, Jalna, Jalna...)

Later, as she walked back towards the town and the liquor
store, Harriet found that the words and phrases she'd deciphered
so painstakingly had, in fact, stuck in her mind. She was going
over the scene in her head when Hope caught up with her.

"What are you doing here?" Hope said breathlessly. "Sandy
said you'd be going for another hour."

"I guess we were all visibly exhausted," Harriet said. "It was
pretty intense. I've never done anything like that before."

"But is it working for you?" Hope asked.

"I think so," Harriet said cautiously, and was spared the need
to elaborate because they had reached the mall and Blanche
called them over.

"Would you like to buy a painting?" she asked Harriet.

Harriet shook her head, not feeling the need to explain that
her itinerant lifestyle was not conducive to art-collecting.
Blanche looked not very optimistically at Hope.

"What's it for this time?" asked Hope. "The car?"

"The car's running fine," Blanche said. "He needs it for gas
to take a trip up to Lac La Ronge."

"What kind of painting is it?" asked Hope.

"A landscape. Watercolor. Two hundred dollars," Blanche said.

"I don't need another prairie landscape," Hope said, "but I wouldn't mind another orb."

"Don't know if I can find one," Blanche said, handing them both cups of coffee and waving away the money Hope was taking out of her purse. "It's a bit stale. I'm just packing up."

As they sat on a bench, drinking the coffee and watching Blanche pack up her cart, Hope explained that Blanche lived with an elderly painter.

"Archie McIntyre. Perhaps you've heard of him."

"Lives with him?"

"Well, it's a kind of commune, actually. He needs looking after and someone has to see that he gets enough food and not too much drink. It's a ménage à trois at the moment. Toby, the mime, lives with them. You might find it a congenial place to live yourself. Just kidding! They'd probably be quite glad to see you, though. Especially if they think you might buy a painting."

"And he still paints, the elderly painter?"

"Well, painting takes place, but how it gets done and who exactly does it is another question. It's mainly watercolours now. Quite pleasant abstract things sometimes. I often wonder if she does them and he just signs them, or if they're the result of a communal effort. People will buy anything with his signature on it. One time he did a picture of the McIntyre tartan for his mother, who been nagging him for years to paint something 'nice.' He included it in one of his shows as a joke and it caught the eye of a rich lawyer who collected art. As a result, Archie got a lot of commissions for similar ones. He made a bundle, apparently, and you see them in boardrooms all across the country. *Royal Stewart, Hunting Stewart, Black Watch* — he did them all on demand. But it's mostly the early stuff that's valuable. You'll see his orbs all over the place, acquired honestly or dishonestly. There's a fine one in the drugstore over there. People acquired them because it made them feel they were connoisseurs of art, having pictures on their walls by someone whose work was hung in the national gallery. Their own homegrown genius. And reassuringly crazy, too, just as geniuses are supposed to be."

"And is he?" Harriet said.

"Is he what?"

"A genius and crazy!" Harriet said.

"Well, you can decide that for yourself," Hope said. "You're bound to run into him before too long."

VIII

Harriet had dreaded telling Hope that she'd found an apartment to rent and wondered briefly if she should try to pass Lilian off as an aunt. But she decided to make a clean breast of it, and Hope didn't even ask the details but simply offered to help her with the move. Harriet was so relieved that she cast aside her reservations about letting Hope see the place and gratefully accepted her assistance. After all, she told herself, where she chose to live was hardly a secret she could expect to keep from Hope for long.

She had so few possessions that the move was accomplished with a few trips up and down the stairs at the rooming house and at the house in Fortescue Street. When they'd finished, Harriet invited Hope to go up and look at the attic.

"Oh, I've already seen it," Hope said. "You were wise, Harriet, not to want to move in with me. It would have been too much togetherness, and I regretted it as soon as I'd asked you. You'll be fine with Lilian, and while you're putting your stuff away, I'll go and have a word with her."

When Harriet came downstairs she found Lilian sitting at a large drafting table. It was covered with newspapers, over which she seemed to have been toiling with a magnifying glass, pens, and scissors. Hope was cutting a piece out of one of the papers and talking to Lilian at the same time.

"I'm always struck by these dietary recommendations — five portions of fruit and vegetables a day. Doesn't say if the amount varies according to weight or size. Same five portions for a woman of five feet and a man of six foot five. The only time they make it gender-specific is when it comes to alcohol. Why is there always this urge to police the behaviour of women?"

"You have a point there," Lilian said, "but that's not the article I wanted cutting out. It's the one on the other side. It's maddening that my hands choose to seize up just when there's so much valuable material in the paper." The headline of the article in question was "Querulous Passenger Kicked Off Cruise Ship." Hope cut it out carefully and passed it to Harriet:

KETICHAN, Alaska. A 73-year-old Maryland woman accused crew members of a cruise ship of serving dinner with paper napkins. Then she said they were calling passengers' attention to non-existent whales. Finally, Captain Dana Lewis decided he'd had enough. When his ship, *Queen of Alaska*, arrived in this southeast Alaska port, he ordered Esther Finegold of Baltimore to pack up and get off his ship. Police were called after Ms. Finegold refused Mr. Lewis's order to leave the ship. She also refused to pack her things when police informed her that she had to leave the ship. Given the choice of leav-

ing peacefully or going to jail, Ms. Finegold still
refused. She was charged with first-degree crim-
inal trespass as a result and taken off the ship.

"I say good for her," said Lilian, and set it beside another
jagged clipping with the headline "Ceiling Falls on Guest in
Palace Mishap."

LONDON. A chunk of moulding fell from a
Buckingham Palace ceiling during a royal
awards ceremony yesterday, injuring one guest
and showering the others with plaster. Despite
needing six stitches to close a head wound,
Nick Howell took the whole event in his
stride. "I'm fine, absolutely fine," he said, standing in a suit covered with plaster and a blue
shirt splattered with blood. Mr. Howell, 28, was
in the palace ballroom to see his father become
an Officer of the Order of the British Empire.
A gilded plaster moulding of decorative fruit
and foliage dropped from the ceiling, hitting
him and raining plaster on his brother. The
Queen looked up but continued with the ceremony. Palace officials and first-aid staff rushed
to carry Mr. Howell from the ballroom. A
spokesman for the palace called it a "terribly
unfortunate and inexplicable accident." .

"Do you see the connection?" Lilian asked them.

"The Queen of Alaska and the Queen of England?" Harriet said.

"No, no, Harriet," Lilian said. "Don't you see? Here you have the forces of authoritative repression — the captain and the queen — and these two different reactions to them. Wonderful Esther Finegold takes a stand against all the outrageous tom-foolery that's going on. Paper napkins indeed! I should like to write and congratulate her. And this pathetic, misbegotten Howell kowtows to all the humbug. At the very least, he should have sued. Howell versus Regina."

Neither Harriet nor Hope felt like arguing the point.

"Do these both go into the 'Blithering Idiot' file?" Hope said. It seemed to be a complicated filing system, but Lilian looked quite satisfied once the clippings were properly stowed away.

"It's quite a ritual, Lilian and the papers," Hope explained when they were back in the car. "You'll probably be called on for assistance on days when her arthritis gets bad. Not to worry, it's a straightforward task, just a matter of cutting out articles and putting them in the right files."

"Does she run a clipping service?" Harriet asked, thinking that it was an ideal job for a shut-in.

"Not a service, exactly. She does it for herself. She feels there has to be some means of reprisal against politicians beyond the mere casting of a vote, and that their follies shouldn't be washed away by time but preserved forever."

"But those weren't political articles you cut out," Harriet said.

"Well, politics is just one part of it. She collects other aspects of human folly. You'll get the idea soon enough. Her work — as she calls it — has its uses, though. People are always calling on her for help when they're trying to trace articles that appeared years ago. It's a regular resource center she's got there."

"And she's been doing it for a long time?"

"For as long as I've known her, but her technique has evolved. Before she lost her mobility, she'd spend hours every day in the legislative building. They have the biggest collection of newspapers in the city — ones from all over the world as well as from all across Canada. She used to copy everything out by hand that interested her. Then Xeroxing came in. It was a turning point in her life, and she started her filing system then. But, of course, photocopies fade. It was never an infallible system. When the arthritis got worse, and she couldn't get over there even in a motorized wheelchair, she took out subscriptions to various papers. And friends drop off papers and magazines when they've finished with them. You've noticed that big stack of newsprint in the hall."

"Poor old soul," said Harriet.

"Well, the new system has its advantages. The available quantity of reading material is smaller, but she has an excellent way of retaliating when she objects to the editorials. She can cancel the subscriptions."

"Doesn't that drive the distributor crazy?"

"It drives a lot of people crazy, especially those who get stuck with returning the copies that come along after she's cancelled. She returns them and demands a refund. Try not to get stuck with the job of running errands to the post office."

"I thought my responsibility for the papers ended with putting them in the dumpster."

"They get recycled now," Hope said. "You have to put out a blue box one day a week at the curbside. But don't worry, she won't make you do anything you don't want to. She's a dear old thing, loved by everyone."

"Everyone?"

"Yes, everyone. She was an excellent music teacher in her day, and she taught almost everyone in town. If she didn't teach them, you can bet she taught someone in the family. That attic of yours was her studio, and kids from all over the city and even from places as far away as the U.S. border have clambered up those stairs to your apartment. The dais where you have your bed was built for her grand piano. Then ... well ... it all came to an end."

"How sad," said Harriet. "What exactly is her illness?"

"Some degenerative disease, a form of rheumatism."

"And the nephew looks after everything?" asked Harriet, wondering if she'd have to be approved by him as well as by his aunt, and if he'd want to increase the rent.

"Ah, the nephews," said Hope. "Their name is Legion. I guess it's a big family."

"But she mentioned just one nephew. The one who paints the dumpsters."

"The one who painted the dumpsters died a few years ago," said Hope.

"Oh god, then she is a little mad!"

"The longer you know her, the less mad she seems," Hope said. "She simply operates on a different system from most of us."

"So you've known her a very long time?"

"One of the joys of living in a town this size," said Hope, "is that the events of people's lives quickly become general knowledge. Privacy is a precious commodity here and something you have to make a concerted effort to maintain. Well, you grew up here, you should know."

"But I grew up in Garlic Heights on the wrong side of the tracks, and we weren't important enough for our shenanigans to arouse anybody's interest."

"Hm," said Hope. "By the way, speaking of privacy. The curly-haired guy you went off with, was he a new acquaintance or an old one?"

Harriet flinched and felt the blood rush to her cheeks.

She'd been in the bookstore standing on one of the kick stools that customers use to reach the high shelves or to sit on and browse. She'd just reached up and taken a book from the top shelf, when she was startled by a voice behind and below her.

"So Harriet is back in town withal."

Of course, she'd known it would happen eventually. It was the first thing she thought of when she knew she was returning to the province, and she'd thought about it regularly since then. But she'd imagined it quite differently — catching a glimpse of him in the audience, for instance, and losing track of her lines. It was the kind of thing he would do — unaffectedly, generously, appreciatively — turn up to see her in a play and then come around afterwards to tell her how good she was. Perhaps send flowers — that was like him too. She'd hoped he would do that so she'd be warned and prepared for her first glimpse of him.

But it was in the bookstore, after all. She gravitated there often, lingering in the pleasant interior, enjoying the soothing quiet, the classical music, the scattering of comfortable armchairs for browsers. On this particular day, however, she'd marched in purposefully and headed up the curved staircase at the back of the store to the biography section, knowing exactly what she wanted. It was the day after she got her first paycheque, and she decided to buy the book she'd been reading bit by bit on her previous visits. It was *O'Keefe and Steiglitz: An American Romance*. She was glad, at such a moment, to have a thick book to grip tightly, though it got in the way awkwardly when he held out his hand to help her step down. It was a freckled hand almost as familiar as her own.

"*An American Romance*," he said, examining the book to give her time to recover.

He looked much the same, young for his age, his hair still red with only flecks of grey around the temples, lots of freckles. He'd gained weight, his face filled out a bit, but it suited him and gave him a cherubic look, like a middle-aged Dylan Thomas. His style of dress was just the same too — casual, boyish. He was wearing a T-shirt of some greenish color, khaki pants, and an open jacket, all shades of green and beige and gold. It was herself she worried about, knowing she hadn't aged so well. Moreover, she was untidy, her hair unwashed and uncombed, her pants unpressed, everything dishevelled and in disarray.

"The director's from Georgia O'Keefe country," she said.

"Ah, the director," he said. "I should have known you were here for a play."

Later he told her that he'd seen her enter the bookstore (he'd recognize her erect posture anywhere) and followed her as she threaded her way between the bookshelves, up the spiral staircase, and to the biography section.

"Where I finally cornered you," he said "You certainly seemed preoccupied."

"We just finished a rehearsal," she said.

Once outside, they got down to the crucial details. He was still living in Saskatoon but he drove down often for meetings with the engineering department. "We liaise with them," he said. Sometimes they met in a small-town midway between the two campuses. Davidson. When he was in town, he stayed at the old Hotel Saskatchewan, preferring it to the newer ones. He was, he said, "still married."

"And you, Harriet?"

"Still not married."

"But not alone?"

"At the moment, yes, alone."

Close up, he looked older than he'd seemed at first. There were wrinkles round his eyes, too, and marked declivities around his mouth. It was the freckles and the curly hair that made him seem young. When they reached the park, he stopped and nodded in the direction of the hotel.

"Do you want to come in?" he said. Just "come in," not "come in for a drink," she noted.

"Not this time," she said. Not "I'm afraid I can't," or simply "No." Her refusal had more to do with hygiene, with the presence of a safety pin in underwear that needed mending as well as washing, things like that. And needing to think things over, assess the situation. And the fact that she was so nervous her palms were sweating. But what she implied, without thinking about it, was "I'll come in next time." Already, she'd acquiesced.

"I'll come down next weekend," he said. Not "I have to come down next weekend" or "I could come down next weekend," she remembered when she went over the conversation afterwards.

"Well, good," she said.

"I'll see you then," he said.

It had happened before in exactly this same way between them, as if they had no will in the matter. They came together, without seeming to exercise any conscious control over their actions or intentions, as if they hypnotized and paralyzed each other. And for her, at least, it had always been disastrous. More than disastrous. Totally catastrophic.

There was some business of writing down telephone numbers, a comment about what time he generally arrived, a question about an answering machine, a suggestion that she should call the hotel if he didn't manage to reach her by a certain time, and then they went their separate ways. For a moment she thought he might reach over and kiss her, but he just smiled, turned, and walked across the park in the direction of the hotel.

The only time they'd touched was when he handed her down off the kick stool, although she'd felt the pressure of his hand on her back when she went ahead of him out of the glass door. She turned back toward the mall, thinking that she had left *An American Romance* on the kick stool in the bookstore, and that she would go back, retrieve it, and take it to the counter. Then she decided she didn't really want it. It would be a distraction when she should be immersing herself in the script. So she reversed directions again, realizing that she didn't know where she wanted to go. She was wondering if he still said "Off, off, you lendings" when he took off his clothes. She was totally spun round and badly in need of a drink.

The whole episode had taken about ten minutes, fifteen at most, and yet it had been observed. Hope had either seen it or heard about it. Harriet felt violated. She wondered if it had been obvious even to a casual observer that it was no chance encounter but a momentous one. Then again, Hope was no casual observer. In any case, she had no intention of explaining to Hope just how momentous it was.

"He's an old acquaintance," she said. Hope seemed content to let it go at that.

IX

"Does he know?" her aunt had asked over the phone.

"Who?" asked Harriet.

"This guy you've been with."

She was nineteen years old, and it was the last time she'd stayed with her aunt. The trip had been hurriedly arranged during her second year in college. It was the same apartment overlooking English Bay that she'd stayed in seven years earlier, and the same steady rain, but everything else was different. This time she took the plane out to Vancouver. She'd called her aunt without telling her mom and dad, and her aunt sent the plane ticket immediately by courier. Aunt Nina was even more tense than she was.

"Look, I don't want to hear any of the details," she said. "We'll get it over with and it will be just as if it never happened."

There was only one thing she wanted to know, and that was the first thing she'd asked when they talked on the telephone.

"Does he know?"

"No," said Harriet, "I haven't told him yet."

"Well, that's a relief," Aunt Nina said. "Whatever you do, don't tell him. It will only complicate matters. I know you're upset, but keep that one thing in your head. You'll get the plane ticket first thing in the morning, and all you have to do is take a cab to the airport and board the plane. I'll do the rest. Just don't say a word to anyone. And don't tell a soul where you're going."

She held up pretty well for two days, assuming that when she got there she'd be able to collapse and cry on her aunt's shoulder and talk about it. She wanted to explain that he really was a neat guy who hadn't made her do anything she didn't want to. It had just happened, and it was the first time for him, too. She was sure if he knew he'd do everything he could to help. But her aunt wasn't having any of that. There was no discussion about what she would do. It had already been decided, and all the arrangements had been made. She had so many questions she wanted to ask about what it would be like and how much it would cost, but her aunt swept them all aside.

She met him in the drama course she'd drifted into merely because she'd heard it was a snap course and it fit into her schedule. Then, quite unexpectedly, she became completely stage-struck. Maybe she wasn't stage-struck, exactly, and certainly not in the same way as her sister, who craved attention and loved twirling and cavorting on the ice in a blue spotlight. What excited Harriet was being drawn into the hermetic world of the play. She'd been a reader ever since her first trip to the west coast, and she could lose herself so completely in a book that when she finished it she felt cut adrift, as if everyone she cared about had died and left her on a planet with aliens. She wanted to go back into the book, crawl between the lines on the pages, and live with the characters.

At the same time as she became a reader, she discovered that books didn't just appear, suspended in a vacuum, but were written by actual human beings about other human beings and connected to real people and places. So the life of the book didn't end when you finished it; it went on and on, and there were hundreds of different ways of getting back inside and exploring what was between the covers. She didn't know the word "context," much less the phrase "*hors de contexte,*" and she happily sought out pictures of the author and the author's house, and saw the movie if there was one based on the book. And she talked about the author and the characters the way her friends talked about movie stars and her mother gossiped about the neighbours.

She loved reading so much that she expected to do well in her freshman English course, but the professor gave her D's and told her to concentrate on a close reading of the text and not get distracted by biographical details about the writer's life, which he called "extraneous matter." But her fascination with "extraneous matter" was too deeply rooted to break off at a moment's notice. And trying to do what he said reduced the "texts" to dry, one-dimensional entities and took all the joy out of reading.

It was the drama course she'd slipped into accidentally that provided the excitement she was used to. There, you could say whatever you thought about the author and the characters without being ridiculed or penalized. Interpretation was a cheerful communal effort, and relating the play to your own experiences was permitted. She enjoyed the class so much it was like discovering reading for the first time. At the end of the course, she tried out for a student production of *A Merchant of Venice* and landed the role of Portia. Her classmates were astonished because she'd only taken the one course. She loved the role and the play and belonging to the community of student actors. When they met each other in the cafeteria, they spoke a special language.

"How now and good morrow, Harriet!"

"Marry, that lecture was passing dull."

"It hath made me thirsty for a butt of sac withal."

He sat beside her in class, a good-natured red-haired farm boy, still sunburned from helping with the harvest. Like Harriet, he was tall and lanky, and friends said they might pass for brother and sister if it weren't for their different colouring. His name was Edward Priestley, and everyone called him Ted. He didn't have a part in the play, but that didn't bother him because he was an engineering major and preferred helping out with the sets and the stage lighting. He could fix anything mechanical. Harriet thought he could have been an actor, too, because he was such a good mimic, always doing some professor or prominent politician and getting the accent just right. He came to all the rehearsals, helped her learn her lines, and soon they were inseparable. It was the happiest time of her whole life — being part of the cast of a Shakespeare play and knowing that, when it ended, she could go on and be part of the cast of another one. The theatre department was away from the rest of the campus in an old red-brick building that you reached by walking across the park. They always walked hand in hand, and everything was lovely until disaster struck.

All this she wanted to tell her aunt, though she knew Aunt Nina wouldn't like the idea of her being an actress. Since she'd helped with her tuition fees, her aunt's prescription for amounting to something had grown a lot more specific. It wasn't just a college degree you needed, but you had to go on to law school after that. So her aunt wasn't ready to hear how well she was doing in drama.

"You just rest and leave it all to me," she said. She gave Harriet books and magazines to read and wouldn't let her leave the apartment. It wasn't until it was over and she was lying on the couch recovering that her aunt had been her old self again. It was a Sunday afternoon, though Sunday mostly seemed like any other day in Vancouver. But when they went to the doctor's office early in the morning she'd heard church bells ringing in the distance and thought of her mum and dad sitting side by side in church without the faintest idea where she was. It had been raining when they set out, but when they came back the rain had stopped and the sun was shining. She thought it was odd that in British Columbia the weather swung so abruptly between the two extremes, the grey rain and the bright sun echoing a person's moods like stage lighting in the theatre.

All the time she was recovering, the sun stayed out. Even though it was March, it was like spring when they walked along the streets around the apartment. All the flowers were coming out, and the trees had pink blossoms on them. Aunt Nina became very cheerful, and it was just like she said — as if it had never happened.

They sat having coffee in the window of the Sylvia Hotel, looking out at the sea, watching the scavenger birds dodging cars to pick scraps of food off the road, and human scavengers picking through the wire garbage cans on the sidewalk.

"Did it cost a lot of money?" she asked.

"Plenty," her aunt said.

"Tell me how much it cost, and I'll pay you back when I can."

"I can afford it, Harriet, so don't worry about that. The best way you can pay me back is to do well in your studies and keep your eye on the ball from now on. And go and see a lady doctor as soon as you get home. You don't want this happening again."

Harriet didn't say anything. She didn't want to talk about Ted and her life at university any more. She just kept looking at the sun sparkling on her aunt's emerald and diamond ring.

"You've got another day before you go back. Is there any-thing you want to do? I think we owe it to ourselves to have some fun. I can get the day off and we could go over to the island."

"I'd like to see a play."

Her aunt suggested a musical, but Harriet wanted to see something in one of the small playhouses. There was a production of *Macbeth* as part of a Shakespeare festival, so they went to that. It was a good performance, but the extraordinary thing about it was that Lady Macbeth was so obviously pregnant. At first Harriet thought that the woman playing the part really was pregnant. She assumed that it was an accident and the director had decided to make the best of it by incorporating it into the role, just as they had when the actor playing Shylock went skiing and came back with a broken ankle. The limp got incorporated into Shylock's repertoire of mannerisms and it worked pretty well.

Then she began to understand that the single detail of Lady Macbeth's pregnancy threw a whole new light on the play and changed her focus on it. She came to see that there was as much about childbirth and childbearing and losing children in the play as there was about murder and death. When it came to the sleep-walking scene, Harriet thought perhaps Lady Macbeth had lost the baby, and that was what pushed her over the edge. She was wearing a flowing gown in the later scenes and seemed less pregnant than she had in the earlier ones.

Everyone knew that Macduff was "from his mother's womb untimely ripped" and that mothers in those days couldn't survive Caesarian deliveries. It must have been a horrendous procedure, cutting the child out of the mother's uterus. Was it significant that the mothers of Macduff and Julius Caesar had died in childbirth? Did not having mothers turn them into ruthless soldiers? She wondered if Shakespeare's mother had died in childbirth.

By the time the final curtain came down, Harriet was convinced that the pregnancy was a stroke of genius on the part of the director. Lady Macbeth had already lost one child, and that she could be involved in murder when she was carrying another made her unbelievably monstrous. On the other hand, it made her ambition more plausible in that she was doing it not just for her husband but also for their kid. This was the kind of thing she would discuss for hours with Ted over coffee in the cafeteria or over beer in the Lazy Owl.

"Do you still like wine, Harriet?" her aunt asked when they got home. It was the first time she'd referred to their holiday years ago on the island.

"Sure," said Harriet, and they sat drinking white wine and looking out at the view.

"I never remembered that Lady Macbeth had a baby, did you?" she asked.

"Now you listen to me, Harriet," her aunt said, her face going taut. "You stop that right now. It's over. You're nineteen years old and you have your whole life in front of you. You can make something of yourself. You can even have a family, too, in the fullness of time. These days women can do anything. You can have it all."

In the fullness of time, she thought. *What a funny expression.*

For the rest of her life, whenever she heard that phrase it always delivered the same quick electrical jolt followed by a slow aftershock of disconnected images — the look on her aunt's face when she spoke the words; the rounded belly of Lady Macbeth; Old Father Time, blindfolded and in rags; and the crows on the road outside the window of the Sylvia Hotel.

Harriet knew her aunt was furious that the play, meant to be a distraction, had brought up the one subject she'd been trying to get Harriet's mind off. She couldn't wait to leave

Vancouver and get away from her aunt, and she felt very guilty about being so ungrateful.

When she got back to her room in the university residence, there were phone messages taped all over the door. Some were from Ted and some were from her mother telling her to call home immediately. "Immediately" was two days earlier. When she finally called, the phone was answered by a neighbour who was there keeping an eye on things.

"Where've you been? They've been going crazy trying to find you, and they're about ready to call the RCMP."

"What for?" she said.

"Your dad's had an accident and he's in the hospital. You'd better get there as fast as you can before it's too late."

So it wasn't over. It had only just begun, and it went on for months. One part of her mind said it was a coincidence, the two things happening at the same time. But another part, especially in the middle of the night, said the events were linked in a pattern of sin and retribution, just like in a Shakespeare play. When she'd been lying on the table in the doctor's office in Vancouver, a car had swerved on a country road hundreds of miles away. She couldn't stop thinking about it. She seemed to remember through the haze of drugs that a voice had said, "There goes a little prizefighter," and another faraway distant voice had said, "It's over now."

Well, it was all over for her father, and no one in the family thought it was strange that she was distraught, because they all knew how close she was to him. She was too upset to finish the semester, and someone else took her part in the play they were doing. Most of her professors were sympathetic and gave her incompletes, but she knew she'd never go back and finish the courses. Her aunt tried to talk to her several times, and Ted never stopped calling and sending letters. She read the letters before she burned them, but she wouldn't go to the phone and talk to him, and eventually he gave up on her.

The big crack-up came six months down the road in August, when the neighbours were all helping them harvest the crop her dad had planted. Years later she learned that gestation goes on in the body and the mind simultaneously, and that a reaction at the end of nine months is common, even when a pregnancy hasn't been carried to full term. Apparently it doesn't get through to the mind immediately that the process has been diverted, and it just keeps running along on the same track it started on with conception. But nobody warned her about that at the time. How could they when nobody except her aunt knew what she'd done?

A few years later when she'd met up with Ted again in Saskatoon, he'd asked her about what happened.

"That time your dad died, did it make it worse that we'd been sleeping together? I was worried that you felt guilty, and that made you crack up."

"Don't be silly," she said. "He didn't know we were sleeping together, so why should I feel guilty? If I was guilty at all, it was because I wasn't there when the accident happened."

"Where were you, anyway?" he said. "You never told me where you were going."

"My aunt had to go to the hospital unexpectedly for an operation, and I made a quick trip out to see her," she said.

"Well, then it wasn't your fault you weren't home."

"No."

So when Hope sprang that question about whether the curly-haired guy was a new acquaintance or an old one, Harriet flinched and felt the blood rush to her cheeks.

X

Harriet was in her room thinking that Sandy's method for learning and remembering her lines had worked out brilliantly for her. Usually she laboured over a script, as if she were cramming for an exam — the kind where you know everything the day before you take it and forget everything the moment it's over. But this time when she picked up the script again she found that whole scenes were already deeply embedded in her mind as if they'd always been there.

MAZO: Do you remember once you said we're too old to build our lives around our play?

CARO: Of course we can build our lives around our play. We did so once and we'll do so again.

MAZO: You wounded me to the quick when you said that. But you spurred me on to greater effort. I tried to make our play so vivid and alive that it would chase out of your head all thoughts of leaving me.

CARO: And you succeeded. Gloriously. You made it so good that nothing could rival it for excitement. For years and years, through sickness and misery and pain, it's always been there. A wonderful safe world of our own.

MAZO: And it can save us again!

CARO: From what?

MAZO: From poverty. From you having to go to work in an office full of men ... Caroline, I had an idea today. Do you remember how you used to read Mr. Galsworthy's books to my mother?

CARO: How could I ever forget. Those awful Forsytes night after night. They come back to me in nightmares.

MAZO: Mr. Galsworthy made a lot of money writing about those awful Forsytes. He also won the Nobel Prize. And that's given me an idea. Why don't I write about the Whiteoaks?

CARO: I can think of hundreds of reasons why not. It's a private play. We'd be exposed. We'd look ridiculous. Then again, who would be interested? We love Renny and Alayne and Finch and the rest of them, of course. But that's because we've known them so long they seem like members of the family. But other people might just prefer the Forsytes.

MAZO: Carolyn, today when you were at work I lay down and closed my eyes and saw the Whiteoaks' manor. Then I opened my eyes, sat up, and wrote down what I saw. Listen:

Jalna looked very mellow in the golden sunlight, draped in its mantle of reddening Virginia creeper and surrounded by freshly clipped lawns.... A pear tree near the house had dropped its fruit on the grass, where it lay richly yellow, giving to the eyes of a town dweller an air of negligent well-being to the scene. It was a day of thick yellow autumn sunshine. A circular bed of nasturtiums around two old cedar trees burned like a slow fire.

Of course the lines were familiar to Harriet. They did come out of a previous existence. She'd known that passage by heart since she was thirteen. She'd been enchanted by it then, and she was enchanted by it now. It wasn't just the words on the page but what was behind them. They described a house in a story she was reading, and they also described a house in a photograph she'd looked at. It was where the writer of the story lived with her daughter. And that daughter ...

Harriet's train of thought was interrupted by a commotion in the rooms below. There'd been noise for some time, but it now rose beyond the level usually associated with Mrs. Pike's efforts to deploy the vacuum cleaner and Lilian's resistance to those efforts. And, she remembered, it wasn't one of Mrs. Pike's days. When she heard Lilian shouting, "No, no, no," in an increasingly desperate voice, Harriet decided it was time to intervene.

The person standing over Lilian appeared to be one of the human scavengers who rummaged through the alley dumpsters. He hovered threateningly, like a great bear, and for a moment Harriet thought he was going to strike Lilian. Then he noticed Harriet in the doorway, grunted, turned away, and shambled off.

"How frightening," said Lilian. "For a moment I thought he was going to hit me. It isn't like him to be so aggressive, but he's been drinking. He can't drink, never could, and he shouldn't drink. He wouldn't harm me, but these rampages are quite alarming all the same."

She started to fuss with the tea-maker, but her hands trembled so much that Harriet had to step forward and help.

"He wanted his picture back," Lilian explained. "This happens periodically. Every few years he tries to reclaim it. He says it's the best thing he's done and, of course, he's right. It's one of the earliest ones, done in his first burst of inspiration. After that he started churning them out whenever he needed money. They got very mechanical, sort of mass-produced."

So, this was Archie. Harriet, who had never actually been into Lilian's bedroom, had several times caught glimpses of the picture when the doors were open to the room that adjoined the sitting room. She'd seen the bed and noticed the large framed painting of an orb that hung above it. She hadn't thought much about it, since Hope said many people in town owned one. She also recalled Hope saying that most of them had been acquired dishonestly, or by taking advantage of the artist.

"This time he says he's having a retrospective and he wants to borrow it for that. I don't know how true that is, but if he got hold of it I might never see it again. The fact is I've had it so long I can't bear to part with it. I don't think I can live without it. Besides, Harriet," Lilian said, sounding as if she was trying to justify hanging on to it, "the painting's safe with me, because when I die it will go to the art gallery and be preserved forever. He'd be just as likely to sell it to some unscrupulous person for the price of a tankful of gasoline or a bottle of Scotch whisky."

Harriet asked if she might look at it.

It was very much like all the others she'd seen — a central image of a circle, created by scraping enamel over a painted masonite surface, placed within a square border. But standing in front of it at the edge of the bed, in the darkened room, induced a kind of vertigo. The puzzle was not so much why Lilian didn't want to surrender it as how she could live on such intimate terms with it. A large mirror opposite the bed caught the picture's reflection so that it must have been the last thing she saw every night before she closed her eyes. She slept between the two overpowering images. It struck Harriet that it was a bit like Bernhardt's habit of sleeping in an open coffin.

"I didn't actually buy it, but I did earn it," Lilian said from the other room. "Anyway, I'm not about to let it go."

Harriet came back and sat down, eager to hear how Lilian had acquired the picture, but before she could ask about it, they were interrupted by a knock at the door.

"That'll be him," Lilian said, and Harriet realized that she had expected him to return.

"Can we come in, Lilian?" a voice cried, and Blanche walked into the room steering a sheepish-looking Archie.

"Yes, you can, and yes, you may," Lilian said sternly.

"He's come to apologize," Blanche said, though Archie showed no inclination to do so, and instead glared resentfully in the direction of the bedroom door, which Harriet had closed behind her. Blanche was carrying a bunch of scraggly daisies that she must have plucked hurriedly from a neighbour's garden as they walked along the street.

"I can't keep an eye on him all the time," Blanche said. "I have to go to work, and Toby does too. So he gets into stuff, and then gets out." She spoke as if he was a troublesome animal that had escaped from its cage, though she was holding him very gently by the arm. "Also he might be having a retrospective, and that's got him all excited and riled up."

"That's all very well," said Lilian, "but he can't go around town snatching his pictures off people's walls."

"There's no danger of that," Blanche said, "because he doesn't want most of them. Just *The Void.*"

"Well, he can't have it," Lilian said. "I did come by it honestly, you know. I have proof of ownership."

"She posed for it," said Archie, looking at Harriet defiantly.

"*Stoppit,*" said Blanche, giving him quite a violent nudge.

"Blanche, you're looking awfully thin," Lilian said. "Are you still smoking?"

"Cut down quite a bit," Blanche said, "and I don't inhale, Lilian."

Archie started fumbling with his pockets, as if suddenly reminded that he needed a cigarette, and Blanche gave him another violent nudge. Harriet noticed that the fingers of her right hand, linked through Archie's arm, had the nicotine stains of a heavy smoker.

"Are you playing the piano at all?" Lilian asked.

"A bit," Blanche said. "It needs tuning at the moment."

"Why don't you get it tuned for her?" Lilian asked Archie. "It's the least you could do."

"Anyone want to buy a painting? A watercolour?" Archie asked, again looking at Harriet.

"You know you can come in here and play whenever you want to," Lilian said to Blanche.

"Yes, I know, Lilian. Thank you."

After they left, Lilian said, "It grieves me to think of her wasting her life and her talent looking after him. Her parents are musicians, and she was something of a child prodigy. She played with the symphony when she was seven years old. I can still see her on the platform, playing away as if it was the most natural thing in the world to do. Then when she finished, she looked out at the audience as if she wondered what they were doing there, and why they were so interested in watching her play.

"In some ways she's very much like Archie. Success came to both of them so quickly and so easily, and I suppose they were overwhelmed by it. They never, either of them, developed what was needed to sustain it. And so it all just evaporated — for her and for him. It all just drifted away, and of course her parents were devastated. They blame everyone but themselves. Certainly, they blame me."

"Why would they blame you?" Harriet asked.

"Well, you see, I was her teacher for years. I think they felt I could have done more.... One can almost understand their reaction. They dedicate their whole lives to fostering musical talent where it barely exists — in their students at the conservatory, in their own children. Then quite unexpectedly a genius appears in their midst, but somehow it all gets squandered and lost, so the rift between them is total."

"I don't understand," Harriet said. "Wasn't she their own child?"

"Their children were twins," Harriet said. "Nice boys, but not a jot of musical talent between the pair of them, although it took the parents some time to realize that. If they ever have realized it."

"And Blanche?"

"She was a late-in-life arrival. They'd been unable to have more children for years, and they wanted more, or perhaps they wanted a girl. They'd quite given up when Blanche arrived unexpectedly. In some ways she seemed like a changeling. And in other ways she was the child they'd always wanted."

"Did the boys resent her?"

"To their credit, perhaps to everyone's credit, they didn't. I think she removed the pressure on them to conform to the parents' expectations. I hear they are both professional hockey players. As for Blanche, the parents treated her as parents often treat clever children. And with the usual disastrous results."

"And Archie?" Harriet said, hoping to learn what was between him and Lilian. Lilian was not forthcoming.

"I think all of us place a heavy a burden on the gifted ones among us," she said. "We see that they have all the talent we'd like to have ourselves. So we live vicariously through them and find our fulfillment by latching onto them. And when they fail us, or show weakness in any way, we can't forgive them. We can't believe that anyone would squander what we would give so much to have."

Harriet was not sure whether Lilian was talking about Archie or Blanche.

"Is that how you felt when Blanche gave up her music?" Harriet asked.

"Oh, I saw it coming," Lilian said. "It was there as clear as the nose on your face. The tension. The unhappiness. The nail-biting. The excuses. 'Don't tell Mum I didn't practise.' 'Don't tell Mum I skipped my lesson.' And then suddenly she was gone out of all our lives. No more to any of us than a casual acquaintance we might meet on the street. It was harder on the parents than on the rest of us. They imagine I see more of her than I do. They come to me for news of her."

A few days later, Blanche's mother came by on one of her news-gathering visits. Harriet had formed a preconceived notion of her as a middle-class matron, coiffed, suited, and well-heeled, but Betsey wasn't like that at all. She was girlish herself, quite petite, with a shaggy hairdo, very dowdy and unkempt.

"I gather you know Stephanie," she said after they'd been introduced. Harriet was momentarilty puzzled, and then she remembered that, of course, Blanche was a chosen name and not a given one.

"Does she ever talk about us?" Betsey said.

"Us?" Harriet said.

"Her dad and me."

"Well, I haven't really known her all that long," Harriet said.

It was sad, as Lilian had said, seeing Betsey's effervescence of friendliness towards anyone who had the slightest contact with her daughter. Whenever Harriet ran into her afterwards, Betsey greeted her effusively as if she were an old friend, and always before they parted she slipped in a few questions about Stephanie. Had Harriet seen her? Was she still smoking as much as ever? Was she happy?

And Harriet always said the same thing — that she really didn't know Stephanie at all, but that she seemed very happy.

Of course, that Stephanie was happy was the last thing that Betsey wanted to hear. She didn't want her to be happy, except in the way she, Betsey, defined happiness. What she dreamed of was Stephanie's "getting back on track," which meant returning to the grind she'd escaped from. The concert pianist career was lost, but some lesser version of it might still be retrieved.

XI

To Harriet's relief Hope soon forgot about the curly-
haired fellow. She simply wasn't interested in that aspect of
Harriet's life; her insatiable curiosity homed in on one subject
only — her aunt's connection to Roger Herbert, and by implication to Mazo herself. Even her interest in Mazo was oddly
circumscribed, as Harriet discovered when she finally dug out
her prized photographs and laid them before her. They were
faded and dog-eared, as befits precious heirlooms that have
been packed and unpacked, lost and found again many times
over the years.

There were two photographs of Antoinette/Adeline as a
small child. In one she sported an old-fashioned riding habit —
jodhpurs that curved widely from the waist to the upper thigh,
a tweed jacket, and a large black velvet cap. In another she was
wearing a party dress, with a smocked bodice and lace collar.
The photograph she expected Hope to find really exciting was
of Mazo's house, the model for Jalna. As she set it down Harriet
recited the description of Jalna that she knew by heart:

Jalna looked very mellow in the golden sunlight, draped in its mantle of reddening Virginia
creeper and surrounded by its freshly clipped
lawns.... A pear tree near the house had
dropped its fruit on the grass, where it lay richly yellow, giving to the eyes of a town dweller
an air of negligent well-being to the scene.
Alayne thought that Jalna had something of the
appearance of an old manorial farmhouse, set
among its lawns and orchards. The spaniels
lazily beat their plumed tails on the step, too
indolent to rise.

Hope was not impressed.

"There's just one problem, Harriet," she said. "Mazo wasn't
living in the house in your picture when she wrote that first
Jalna novel. She was living in Gertrude Pringle's rooming house,
remember? It was years after that before she could afford to own
a house like the one in your picture."

"But it corresponds exactly," said Harriet. "Look at the
Virginia creeper and the fruit tree. And the dogs. Did she fix up
the house to look like the one in the novel?"

"Who knows?" said Hope. "It's not uncommon for a
writer's fictional world to take over her mind so completely that
it supplants the real one." She seemed totally unimpressed by the
picture, and Harriet felt that her cherished relics had been
exposed as frauds.

"So you just snitched those out of your aunt's photograph albums?"

"Not hers, no, the ones we'd looked at in the house on the beach I told you about."

They were sitting in Hope's garden drinking tea, on a summer afternoon filled with the smell of fruit.

"Ah, yes," said Hope. "Tell me again about Roger turning up at your aunt's place."

Harriet had already described several times the scene in her aunt's apartment when Roger appeared at the door. Hope invited her for drinks or lunch and then submitted her to a grilling, as if she suspected her of deliberately leaving out a crucial part and was giving her one more chance to remedy the omission. It felt like a courtroom cross-examination, in which the interrogation was intended to reveal a conflict between the testimony she gave today and the one she gave yesterday.

"I already told you, Hope."

"I know. But I've a lot on my mind. I forgot the details. Would you mind if I record it this time?" And she set a cassette player on the table where Harriet had laid out her photographs.

"Well, there was a rapping at the door and my aunt looked startled. As I told you before."

"Why do you think she looked startled?"

"I suppose because she'd told him I'd be there and warned him not to show up, and he'd forgotten."

"Why didn't she want him to show up while you were there?"

"Obviously, she didn't want me to know there was something between them."

"But his dropping in wouldn't necessarily have indicated there was something between them, would it?"

"It showed he had a habit of dropping in. He didn't ring the bell in the lobby, he came right up. He had his own key."

"Did you figure that out at the time?"

"At the time? I don't think so. Not immediately."

"When did you figure it out?"

"I suppose after we got to the island and Aunt Nina started falling apart, things started to come together — the relationship with Roger Herbert, the hatred for Mazo, the grief over the child. Look, Hope, it was forty years ago. I was just fourteen years old."

"Twelve. You were twelve years old."

"So…"

"Yet you have such a clear memory of this meeting."

"Yes. It's the kind of thing that makes an impression — your first encounter with the rich and famous. I knew he was powerful, and so I was curious about him. I expected him to look different, and I was disappointed because he looked just like everyone else. Ordinary."

"But he was kind to you, wasn't he? He didn't just ignore you, or look put out because you were an obstacle to what he'd come for, because you'd interfered with his pleasure?"

"No, not at all. He was nice. He said something about my name. It was the name of his favorite aunt, he said. As if that made it less ridiculous."

"His favorite aunt. Ah! What did you think of that?"

"Well, it annoyed me. I was very self-conscious about my name. I'd always been teased by the kids at school — they called me Hairy and Harikari. So I thought he was being condescending. It didn't make it any better that it was the name of his elderly aunt, who must have been older than God, because he was pretty old himself. And who was he to talk anyway, because he had a silly name too. It was a name in a limerick my friend Fiona used to recite:

There once was a woman called Maud
Who thought that her kids came from God
But it wasn't the Almighty
Who crept up her nightie
But Roger, the lodger, the sod.

Very risqué for grade school."

"Yes, you *were* angry. And you said he mentioned his children?"

"He said his sons were older than me. He said they were away at school, and he asked how I'd feel about leaving my parents and going away to a boarding school."

"That you didn't tell me before."

"I just remembered it. It made my aunt really furious. She said, 'Roger, that's a lot of nonsense.' Obviously, my parents couldn't afford to send me to a boarding school. So it was an insensitive, arrogant question. I just remembered something else."

"Yes?"

"My aunt suddenly said we were low on milk and sent me down to the 'inconvenience store.' There was a store on the corner. We called it that because of the odd hours it opened and shut. So I ran down and it was shut. The Chinese man who owned it used to put a notice on the door: 'I'm coming.' The notice was on the door that day, but it didn't matter because I knew we weren't low on milk. She just wanted me out of the way."

"While they made love?"

"No, no. More like while they had an argument. I thought, 'How dare she be so rude to her boss?' I took my time, and when I got back she looked even more upset, and then he got up to leave. And that was that."

"What was that?"

"The end of it. He shook my hand very courteously and said he'd enjoyed meeting me. I liked that. It made me feel grown up and proud because he was an important man."

"And then you went to the window and watched him go to his car?"

"I've remembered something else before that. He took out his wallet and said a little gal in a big city must see a lot of things she wants to buy. And he gave me a twenty-dollar bill. It was a lot of money in those days. I was so stunned at getting twenty dollars that I forgave him for what he said about my name, and for calling me a little girl."

"Ah!"

Hope switched off the tape recorder. She always seemed satisfied when she pried loose a new bit of information, no matter how inconsequential it was. Then she offered a reward. She knew by now that Harriet drank, so she swept away the tea things and gave her a gin and tonic. Sometimes when Harriet needed a drink she was tempted to invent some detail in order to please Hope.

"I remember the tie," she'd said one day. "It was a most unusual tie. I'd never seen one like it before." But Hope was interested only in what he said and what her aunt said. She wasn't interested in his tie or anything else he wore. Though that wasn't quite true, either. One day, she asked Harriet what her aunt did when he left.

"She went into her bedroom and changed her clothes."

"Were you going out?"

"No, she was changing into the clothes she wore around the house."

"Had you been out earlier?"

"No, we'd been in all day."

"Then she changed her clothes because she was expecting a visit?"

"I suppose so. It was all so long ago. I do remember she went into her bedroom and came out wearing a housecoat. I'm sure of that. But if she'd been expecting him, she wouldn't have been so angry when he turned up, would she?"

"Could there have been another reason why she was angry?"

On that occasion they'd been having lunch, and Hope pressed her to have a brandy with her coffee and picked up the tab. She often did that anyway, but this time Harriet felt she was being rewarded.

Hope's curiosity was distinctly prurient. She'd wanted an exact description of her aunt's bedroom. Harriet had no trouble with that. It was a lovely room with a big picture window over-looking English Bay. Harriet had realized on her second visit that the apartment was far more luxurious than a secretary, even an executive secretary to an important man, could afford. The bed-room was richly furnished with brocade curtains that matched the cushions on the chaise longue and the bedspread on the large double bed. It got so that Harriet could imagine them — Roger and her aunt — lying in it in the afternoon. Or the two of them eating breakfast on the balcony after he'd spent the night there.

Sometimes she thought Hope's obsession was infectious and that she'd caught, incubated, and come down with a bad case of it. She was beginning to brood on the meeting she'd witnessed between her aunt and Roger, as if it were freighted with a sig-nificance she didn't yet understand. Was it some kind of primal scene between the parents of Mazo's daughter, or perhaps the closest Hope could get to the coming together that had pro-duced Antoinette? But that had no direct bearing on Mazo's life. Or had it?

Harriet had the sense that the questions were not random, that they were nudging her towards something to do with the play. There was one scene in particular that Hope and the director were having trouble with. It concerned the episode in which Mazo decided to adopt a child, and it wasn't working because, as Sandy said, it lacked clarity. Harriet wondered if Hope was expecting her to come up with something that would fill out the background and focus the scene.

Was it possible to contemplate that scene so intensely that all its hidden meanings would be revealed? A connoisseur of art, after all, could stare so long at a painting that the figures in the foreground would recede and the background texture clarify until every brush stroke, every half-articulated idea in the painter's mind could leap out. But an incident excavated by memory from the past was different from a scene framed and fixed in oil. Memory was a trickster, playing fast and loose with truth and not above making corrections and adding touches here and there.

Had there been another meeting in the same room, Harriet now wondered, with Mazo present instead of herself? It was very likely. There must have been such a meeting somewhere. Perhaps Roger had arrived with his cousin on his arm. There would have been the same tension, her aunt hostile and defensive, Roger placatory, caught between the two women. Currents would have been going back and forth between the two of them as they exchanged pleasantries.

"Would you care for tea?"

"Please don't trouble yourself, my dear."

"The child will have the best of homes."

"The money will be paid when the child is delivered."

"Delivered...?"

"A clumsy choice of words. Forgive me. When I receive the child."

"Well, then, it's all settled."

"All we have to do now is wait."

"Yes, wait."

Then Roger and Mazo would have left. Perhaps Mazo went ahead, and Roger lingered for a moment to make some consoling gesture, to hug or kiss her, promising to return as soon he could get away. Or perhaps they left together, and Nina walked to the window and watched them get into the car and drive away, and then she went into her bedroom and changed into her bathrobe. And wept. Certainly she wept.

Harriet walked home with her discredited photographs in her pocket, crossing the wooden bridge over the creek that separated Hope's neighbourhood from Fortescue Street. As she walked along, she thought about her aunt and her desire for Harriet to "have it all." She'd wanted Harriet to have all the benefits she'd achieved in her own life, without the liabilities. And it was true that Harriet had broken the cycle of her mother's dreary domestic life and forged a career of sorts for herself. On the other hand, she hadn't perfected her aunt's kind of life; she'd actually replicated it, liabilities and all. She'd had a lover with a family of his own, in whose life she was a mere appendage. She'd been pregnant, but no child would ever call her "Mother," and she had no family except a sister from whom she was totally estranged. Could it be that what she'd witnessed of her aunt's life when she was twelve had somehow shaped the course of her own life?

"Is that you, Harriet?" Lilian called out as she entered the house, and so Harriet went in to talk to her.

"Can I get you anything?" she asked, but Lilian shook her head.

"I have everything I need, Harriet. I just wanted to say that I'm glad you're here. I hope you stay for quite some time. I think this will be a good place for you. A lucky place."

"Thank you, Lilian, I think it will, too," Harriet said, but in a very doubtful voice.

XII

Harriet had developed the habit of dropping in to pass the time of day with Lilian whenever she left the house or returned. Lilian was always ready to put aside her current project, serve tea, and impart one of her unlikely opinions.

"I don't believe in God," she told Harriet one day. "I don't approve of God, but I take a great interest in him all the same. I suppose that's the way most people feel about loyalty. You often hear people refer to 'my favourite hymn.' That's all very well, but I wonder how God feels about that. He probably dreads Sundays and hearing the same dreary songs every week. Maybe he likes flattery, but I doubt it. He's probably saying, 'If I hear "How Great Thou Art" one more time, I'll send down another of my really nasty plagues — boils or frogs. That'll teach them a lesson.' And that lurid twenty-third psalm. 'The Lord is my Shepherd.' Everybody sings it, but nobody thinks about what happens to the sheep. They get slaughtered, of course! Why else does a shepherd look after sheep? It's appalling!"

Harriet usually said, somewhat cravenly, that she agreed with Lilian.

She learned that Lilian's sitting room was the local equivalent of Picadilly Circus, where eventually everyone in the world passes through. New people appeared every day, and sometimes familiar ones reappeared in different guises. One day when Harriet returned home, she heard Lilian talking in her explanatory way and a masculine voice responding. When she popped her head around the door, she was surprised to see Archie sitting there, looking quite tidy and presentable. Lilian had a folder of clippings on her lap, and she was passing them over to Archie one by one. Archie was reading bits of them aloud.

"They're about the National Gallery's purchase of the Barnett Newman painting," Lilian said.

"For my retrospective," Archie said.

"I saw that painting in the National Gallery once," Harriet said. "It was amazing. But isn't he from New York?"

"He is, but he was out here in the sixties," Lilian said. "He's part of the history of this place, but you'll find few people willing to admit that. Or if they do, they think he was a bad influence."

"'Is that all you're aiming to do?' he says to me the first time he sees my paintings," Archie said. "I'd been to Paris and New York and I thought I knew what was going on. At least I thought I did. And he says, 'Is that it?' It's like, Jesus! Wake up!"

"It may surprise you, Harriet," Lilian said, "but this place made its mark on the international art scene."

"It was where it was at," Archie said. "Jesus."

"Briefly," Lilian said. "For one brief moment."

"But what a moment," Archie said. "Jesus Christ."

"And what happened?" Harriet asked.

"I lost it," Archie said ambiguously.

A great deal went on in the house that Harriet wasn't privy to, even though she was well attuned to the noises that rose from below. Some of the visitors played Lilian's piano. One or two played Chopin. Études and nocturnes, like the recital pieces of precocious music students, were rendered over and over; there were pauses between the pieces and sometimes in the middle of them, and Harriet assumed that Lilian was making corrections and suggestions.

And then there was Mrs. Pike.

From the start, Harriet associated Mrs. Pike with increased commotion down below. There was the roar of the vacuum cleaner, accompanied by a growing crescendo of argumentative voices, one of protest and one of insistence. She gathered that the cleaning process was a tug-of-war, and that Lilian was the stronger participant and the winner, because Lilian's rooms never looked much tidier after cleaning days than they did before.

That wasn't the only feature of cleaning days; Harriet gradually became aware of a subtle change in her own quarters on those days. When she returned to her own rooms after rehearsal, things were not in the same places as they were when she left. Cushions were rearranged, dishes in the draining board returned to the cupboards, ones in the sink washed and stacked in the draining board. It was all a little disconcerting, and she tried to broach the matter with Lilian.

"Would Mrs. Pike ever go up and clean my room?" she asked.

"If you paid her," Lilian said, misunderstanding the question. "However, I wouldn't recommend that. But Mrs. Pike has an arsenal of weapons in the hall closet — dirt devils, dust-busters, and so on. You're quite free to help yourself to them. If I were you, I'd just run over the carpets myself. You're all alone up there, and out much of the time. Surely you can't be making much of a mess."

So Harriet let the matter drop. But still, returning to what now felt very much like home, she was aware of a visitation by a benign presence. And really the answer was very simple. On the next cleaning day she returned to hear voices and found Mrs. Pike at the kitchen sink with a soap opera playing simultaneously on both television sets.

"It's just ending," Mrs. Pike said distractedly, but unapologetically, "and then I'll make us a nice cup of tea." By the time Harriet had gone up to the attic, dumped her stuff on the bed, and come down again, the program had ended and the kettle was boiling.

"Does Lilian know you come up here?" Harriet asked as she accepted her cup.

"Lilian knows what she wants to know," Mrs. Pike said. "I can't miss my show. I couldn't come and clean if I had to. Rosalie that lives in the North End said, 'Ma, we can tape it for you and you can watch it when you've had your supper.' She has one of them things where you put tapes in…"

"A VCR," Harriet said.

"It's a blessing you're here, that's for sure," Mrs. Pike said, switching topics. "The poor old soul shouldn't be by herself. They go a bit funny. I said that to Rosalie, 'The poor old thing shouldn't be on her own.' I've seen what happens to them that's left all by theirselves, not that she's in such bad shape as the other one, but you never know. *She* wasn't in such bad shape to begin with, she just got like that with time and neglect and everything. I've said that time and time again. If anything like that happens to me again, that'll be the end of me. It put me in bed for a week, the last time around."

"The last time around?" Harriet said.

"I was the one that found her," Mrs. Pike said. "I come in like I always done in the morning, let myself in the door with my own key that they gave me in case of anything happening, not that they thought anything like that would happen, just that she might lock herself in the bathroom or something. Anyway, I called out to her, I always tried to look on the bright side, she needed cheering up the poor thing, when I heard nothing I thought she must've gone out, though where she would have gone that early I don't know. And I don't know what made me go up to the attic because I never hardly went up there, it's a house just like this with a little staircase and going up the staircase the first thing I seen was the feet, one shoe on and one dropped off. I can tell you my heart stopped pumping when I saw that."

"Good lord!" said Harriet.

"You ever put any of that stuff in your tea?' Mrs. Pike said.

"That stuff?" said Harriet, and then realized that Mrs. Pike had taken note of the bottles of liquor in the cupboard over the sink.

"I come over all funny just thinking about it."

"I can see how you would," Harriet said. "Do help yourself to some." She watched while Mrs. Pike poured some Scotch first in her own cup and then in Harriet's, and waited for her to continue her story.

"Were you in time?" Harriet asked.

"What?"

"The poor old soul that you found in the attic? Did you save her?"

"There wasn't nothing nobody could do to save her. It was too late."

"Was it a long time ago?" Harriet said.

"Feels like it was yesterday," Mrs. Pike said. "You don't forget something like that in a hurry. Drinking all the time she was, not that I've anything against anybody having a drink now and then, but it was loneliness, nobody coming near the place for days on end. At least there's nothing like that with Lilian, and now you're here and that's a blessing just like I told Arla, because you never know. You just never know. But to this day I can't go near that house without coming over all queer. That girl comes up to me on the street one day, as if butter wouldn't melt in her mouth, 'Oh, dear Mrs. Pike, if you could just come in this once, Archie said to tell you he'd be so grateful. Just for a bit of spring cleaning.'"

"What girl?" Harriet said.

"The one that sells sandwiches on the mall, lives with him that's supposed to be a painter. 'Oh yes, and how many springs is it since that place got a good cleaning?' I says, 'And I'd want more than grateful, I'd want paying a proper wage, and not one of them daubs, like he tried to pay me with the last time.' I did for his mother when she was alive, now that was a different matter altogether, she was a real lady. He put her in her grave with his carrying on is my opinion. Well I must be getting off."

She carried the cups and saucers over to the sink, washed them, and set them neatly in the draining board. Harriet had a lot of questions she wanted to ask, but they would have to wait for the next cleaning day.

"I ran into Mrs. Pike today," Harriet said to Lilian later.

"Ah!" said Lilian flatly.

"She was telling me about a tragic accident that happened on the street."

"Well, Mrs. Pike would know all about that," Lilian said.

"She made it sound very sinister," Harriet said.

"I suppose she did," Lilian said. "I'm not sure that this street has seen more tragedy than any other street in a town this size. Of course, Mrs. Pike is privileged by her work to know more about the private lives of our neighbours than most of us do, or want to do. Nor am I sure that Mrs. Pike's knowledge of her clients is informed by understanding. She has a fondness for the sensational and a tendency to exaggerate ordinary events."

"She said the woman killed herself."

"That was a very sad case, yes."

"In Archie's house."

"Yes, it was in Archie's house, but at the time he wasn't living there. The family home had passed into other hands after his mother's death, and it was only later that he came into possession of it again."

Lilian's tone seemed to constitute a rebuke, and Harriet decided that if she wanted more information about the neighbourhood she'd have to seek it elsewhere.

"So Mrs. Pike's been filling you in on the recent history of Fortescue Street!" Hope said with a smile when Harriet asked her.

"It all sounded a bit wild," Harriet said.

"Not nearly as wild as the ancient history," Hope said. "Of course, I'm a relative newcomer, so my version of events is probably even more unreliable than Mrs. Pike's."

"So she is unreliable?" Harriet said.

"Mrs. Pike is an archivist in her own way, just like Lilian," Hope said. "Only where Lilian collects clippings, Mrs. Pike collects stories. Her medium is essentially oral, and the same stories are told so often that they get shaped for dramatic effect. That naturally leads to some distortion."

"So she works for you too?" Harriet said.

"Not any more," Hope said, "at least not regularly. I soon learned that I ran the risk of becoming her material rather than being the recipient of it."

"I was hoping she'd tell me about Lilian and Archie," Harriet said. "I'm curious about their relationship."

"You're not the only one," Hope said. "That's a subject of universal speculation, and the theories about it are numerous. They were childhood sweethearts, high school sweethearts, something like that. Apparently there was a formal engagement at one time, but that was broken off. Lilian, I believe, broke it off."

"Did her family object? Was there a class difference?"

"Not at all," Hope said. "These were early days, long before Archie's decline. The two families were close friends in the beginning. So close, in fact, that one of the more colourful rumours involves incest. Of course, that's the only twist in a story that guarantees shock and horror these days. The parents were a foursome and often travelled together, and they shared a cottage someplace, I believe. All this was before Archie's father was killed on the highway, and that put an end to the foursome. The threesome didn't work, and they went in different directions after that. As for Lilian, she remained in the family home all her life. I've always suspected her interest was not predominantly in men. But I would think that, wouldn't I?"

"Ah. Is that what Mrs. Pike thinks?"

"I think Mrs. Pike's theories tend to run along more conventional lines. Star-crossed lovers, he-broke-her-heart-and-it-never-mended type of thing. But you can ask her yourself, Harriet. She may be more forthcoming with you, especially if you're willing to barter with some juicy details about your own personal life."

"Oh my god," Harriet said.

"Well they don't have to be true," Hope said. "They don't even have to be plausible. They simply have to be grist for the rumour mill."

"Was Lilian an only child?" Harriet said.

"Both she and Archie were," Hope said, "the cherished darlings of doting parents. Why do you ask?"

"I was just thinking. If Lilian had no brothers or sisters, how could she have so many nephews? Is nephew an honorific or something?"

"You'd have to ask Mrs. Pike about that," Hope said.

Harriet saw plainly that Mrs. Pike was an essential source if she wanted to understand the neighbourhood in which she'd found herself. And since she did, she resolved to try to make it home early on Mrs. Pike's visitation days.

XIII

"You don't have to prepare anything or give a lecture," said Hope, "just sit there and answer questions and I'll buy you a slap-up lunch afterwards. And one short hour, that's all it will take."

Now, hast thou but one bare hour to live, thought Harriet.

She hadn't wanted to do it, but Hope was very strong-willed, and on the appointed morning Harriet found herself walking across the park to the old campus and making her way to the drama department. She was early, and Hope was teaching the class before the one Harriet was to address. She peered into the classroom, and since Hope was lecturing she slipped quietly into the back row, mildly curious to see Hope in her professorial role. The student in the next seat automatically placed the text between them with a smiled invitation to share it. Harriet scooted her desk close to the other one and looked over the page:

THE QUEM QUAERITIS TROPE

Interrogatio: Question:
Quem quaeritis in sepulchro, O Christicoloe?
Whom seek ye in the sepulcher, O followers of
Christ?

Responsio: Response:
Jesum Nazarenum crucifixum, O coelicoloe.
Jesus of Nazareth, who was crucified, O angels.

Angeli: Angels:
Non est hic; surrexit; sicut praedixerat. He is
not here; he is risen; exactly as he prophesied.
Ite, nunciate quia surrexit de sepulchro! Go and
tell everyone that he is risen from the sepulchre!

Harriet was familiar with the text, a fragment of dialogue
that contained, implicit as the germ in a grain of wheat, the seed
of modern English drama. Seeing it again threw her back in
time, sharing a book with Ted, her desk comfortably joined with
his, perhaps in this very classroom, perhaps at this very desk on
which someone had carved two hearts with initials and an arrow
stuck between them.

At the front of the class, Hope, who had undoubtedly seen
her come in, didn't acknowledge her. She was explaining that the
three exchanges, an elaboration of the gospel of Mark 16:1–8,
were originally sung antiphonally as part of the Easter service.

She talked about the tripartite structure. Act I: Enter three
women in mouring searching for something. Act II: Problematic
like all second acts, with its exchange of information necessary

to advance the plot, its transitional nature, its dip in action between the peaks of the other acts. Then Act III: The triumphant resolution followed by a summons to action — go forth and tell the world! She pointed out the perfect symmetry of threes and multiples of three echoing the Trinity: three Marys, three Angels, and three scenes corresponding to three events — the crucifixion, the entombment in the sepulchre, and the resurrection on the third day.

Harriet's partner paused in her note-taking and smiled self-consciously because she was uncertain how to spell "symmetry." Harriet took the pencil and wrote the word correctly. She was reminded of Ted's habit of leaning over to scribble messages on her notepad.

Hands rose, questions were called out — some sensible, some foolish, and some intended to impress the teacher — about opera, musical comedy, the Lord's Prayer, the gender of the actors, the absent hero. Hope answered them, irrelevant and relevant alike, in her calm, imperturbable voice, betraying no awareness of Harriet's presence in the back row.

Had she staged this intentionally? It was impossible to avoid the parallel between the Quem Quaeritis and the scene Hope kept making her describe. The door to the Vancouver apartment flung open and the little drama ensuing — the cast of three, the sequence of three events: the arrival of a visitor, the challenge and the explanation, the resolution and departure. And the final command, "You two go forth and enjoy yourselves together on the island!"

Hope's voice droned on in the warm morning about religion and its sacred texts, in which the significance increased as the words were repeated and committed to memory: "Read, mark, learn, and inwardly digest." They condensed an entire system of belief into one brief conversation. A prophecy was fulfilled, a faith justified, a tragedy redeemed, and then a command — go and make these tidings known! More and more meanings seemed to emanate from the text, like ripples moving outwards from the centre to the edge of the pond.

Then, quite suddenly, the bell rang and broke the spell. The ecclesiastical mood had been so heavy that the students might have been expected to bow their heads or cross themselves. Instead they grabbed their belongings unceremoniously, pulled on their jackets, and rushed towards the door. When Harriet turned to say thanks for sharing the book, her neighbour had already slammed it shut and headed for the door. And even as the class disintegrated, another congregation waiting outside surged forward at the first note of the bell, without waiting for the room to empty. Chaos had come again. The two groups clashed and mingled, and pandemonium reigned. It had barely subsided when Hope stood on the podium and said, "We have a distinguished guest with us this morning."

She presented Harriet to the class as a former student who had started out on this same campus just like them. She went on to list all of her theatrical credits, as if Harriet had taken the world by storm, and ended with an account of her role as Sarah Bernhardt, making it seem like the peak of an illustrious career. She talked about the current play as if Harriet were doing them a favour by coming down from Olympus to grace a small provincial theatre with her presence. Then, leaving Harriet in splendid isolation on the dais, she took a seat at the end of the front row and sat back to enjoy the spectacle.

There was a moment of complete silence while thirty pairs of eyes bored into Harriet. She was conscious of her ragged pants, bare feet, wooden clogs, of falling short of the expectations raised by Hope's fulsome words. She should have worn something glamorous and dramatic — stage makeup, a fringed shawl, black stockings, long silver earrings. At that moment she could have strangled Hope for getting her into this spot.

After a while, a hand went up and someone asked about stage fright, and if she had a special trick for remembering her lines. Other tentative questions followed. Harriet talked vaguely about her lapses of memory and about the many unpredictable things that can happen in the course of a performance. Then the serious questions started. How did she prepare herself psychologically for a role? Did she do research or field work, visiting a hospital, a prison, a forest — whatever the role required? How did she resolve conflicts with the director over the interpretations of a role?

"A lot of actors get identified with one particular role," said a girl with a beaded headband across her forehead. "Which of your roles do you feel most identified with?"

"With Sarah Bernhardt," Harriet said without hesitation. "Well, it's not often an actor gets to play another actor, and she was such a magnificent one. She lived with so much bravado on and off the stage. She played whatever took her fancy, regardless of whether she was disqualified by age or sex. She made a mockery of typecasting. She was the only actor who played both Ophelia and Hamlet. And she played Hamlet when she was an old woman with one leg amputated. She played Joan of Arc when she was old enough to be her grandmother."

"And what about your present role? Isn't there a big difference between playing an actor and playing a writer?" Harriet hadn't thought much about that, and the class waited patiently while she tried to frame an answer.

"In some ways they weren't all that different," she said. "They were both sort of illegitimate. Bernhardt was literally born out of wedlock to a kept woman, a courtesan. And she was a Jew in an anti-Semitic country. Mazo's family was less than respectable, and she lived in a same-sex relationship with overtones of incest. They both had to struggle for financial independence and social acceptance, and they each choreographed their lives in a highly theatrical manner as they tried to lay claim to legitimacy."

She took a deep breath and looked at Hope to see if she approved. Hope seemed to be filing her fingernails. "They were both products of the nineteenth century struggling to carve out a role for the female artist," Harriet continued. "Acting came naturally to them because they'd served a long apprenticeship in learning to be a woman — mastering the appropriate gestures and speech, the costumes, the makeup." Now she was regurgitating statements that Hope had made.

"One isn't born a woman, one becomes a woman," offered the girl with the headband. The man beside her, who'd been looking at his watch and generally pantomiming boredom, now yawned mightily, closed his eyes, and didn't open them again for the rest of the session.

"Writing, on the other hand, was a transgressive act, an activity completely off limits for the female sex," Harriet said. "In the nineteenth century women who attempted the pen were thought to be monstrous. So instead of training for a prescribed role and modifying it, Mazo had to create one from scratch."

"Wasn't Bernhardt a writer as well?" the girl with the headband asked.

"She was. But she was a very different kind of writer from Mazo. Bernhardt wrote stage plays for herself to perform, and also a hefty, evasive autobiography. The kind of writing she did meshed with what women did traditionally — using themselves as art and erasing the distance between that art and their life."

"So then Mazo was more daring in the way she took on the male-dominated literary world — is that what you're saying?" the girl asked.

"In a way, yes," Harriet said. "Mazo appeared to live less boldly, and more reclusively, but what she did actually *was* more daring, more potentially dangerous. Remember too that she was living in *fin de siècle* Toronto, which was a much less permissive climate than *fin de siècle* Paris. Toronto wasn't particularly receptive to artistic activity, and certainly not by women."

"So there were more differences than similarities between them?" the girl said.

"One similarity," Harriet said, "was this: they were both so spun round and torn between the roles they desired and the roles society prescribed for them that they both completely lost track of when they were acting and when they weren't —"

Suddenly the bell rang, and chaos returned instantly. Harriet in full rhetorical flight was left standing ignored on the stage. She was chilled by the abrupt withdrawal of attention and felt strangely drained until Hope came to rescue her.

"You're a natural," Hope said when they were having lunch. "That was a brilliant talk you gave on Bernhardt and Mazo. If all else fails, you can teach drama. We're always looking for sessionals."

"All else has failed," Harriet said.

"Well, you could do worse than staying on here," Hope said. "You could cobble together a fair income. A bit of teaching, a bit of radio work, parts in local plays, offering workshops from time to time. And you seem pretty comfortable in your lodgings. Not a bad life."

"You know, about Bernhardt and Mazo," Harriet said, "they really are two sides of the same coin, aren't they? That never struck me before."

"There, you've discovered one of the joys of teaching. No matter how dull and unpromising a class, something happens. I think the sociologists call it a group dynamic. Somebody lobs a question at you, not even knowing what they're asking or where it will lead. And it's like a shot in the vein. It sets you off on a whole new trail. It can be very addictive, teaching."

"It would get to me, though," said Harriet, "the way they all pack up and dash out the minute the bell rings. Leaving you in mid-sentence, and just when you think you've got them in the palm...."

"Yes, it certainly lacks some of the protocols of the theatre. No final curtain, no business with the lights, certainly no applause. It's more like a rehearsal than an actual performance. The old authoritarian guard doesn't stand for that, of course. It's possible to lay down the law."

"But you don't?"

"Not about that. There are other things worth making an issue of. But it's a mistake to reduce them to a passive audience. I like a bit of creative anarchy. If it's too regimented and repressive, the atmosphere gets sterile."

"But that guy that fell asleep. He did it so pointedly, it was like a deliberate insult," Harriet said.

"Ah, Jason," Hope said. "He's the most valuable member of the group. His falling asleep was a mark of respect for you. You're lucky he didn't object to everything you said. He and Bitha — the girl with the headband — often spend the whole hour arguing; I depend on them to keep the class going on days when I've not had time to prepare a lecture."

"Incidentally," said Harriet, "did you do that on purpose — that Quem Quaeritis you were on about when I walked in? It seemed to hit home, somehow."

"Of course it hit home," Hope said. "That's why it's so interesting. All the great dramas of our lives can be reduced and simplified in exactly the same way."

Harriet, swirling the wine in her glass, was a little high and excited about the things that had come up in class.

"I hope you're not gobbling this lunch down mindlessly," Hope said. "This is a very expensive place. And this is not plonk you're drinking, it's a very expensive wine."

"Sorry," said Harriet.

She sensed that Hope's invitation to talk to the class had been a test of some kind, and she felt she'd passed it with flying colours.

XIV

Coming down from the adrenalin rush of the classroom, Harriet thought, was a bit like coming down from the high of the stage. She couldn't stop dwelling on her mistakes, regretting certain remarks, and wishing she'd made others or answered questions differently. Hope was totally uninterested in analyzing the session.

"Let it go, Harriet," she said. "You can always come back another day and talk to them again."

Harriet was so engrossed in her thoughts when she returned home that she went up to her room without making her customary visit to Lilian. She was heading upstairs when she almost stumbled over someone curled up in a ball on the top step of the narrow stairway.

"Why, Blanche, what are you doing here? Is something wrong?"

"Oh, Harriet, I just had to get away from them. It's impossible there just now."

"Well, come on in, and I'll make us some tea — or would you like something else?"

"Is it OK if I smoke, Harriet? Lilian doesn't allow it."

"There are lots of things Lilian doesn't allow, but they seem to be done anyway," Harriet said, nodding at the television set.

"Oh, Harriet, you're so lucky!"

"Lucky?"

"Having your own place and living alone in it and having your work and having your life…."

"But I thought you loved what you do, Blanche."

"Well, I do. Did. But suddenly everything's started to go wrong. It's this retrospective. It's got Archie all riled up. Half the time he's in a crazy manic state, and the other half he's in a rage because they keep asking him questions about his work and his life. And he can't stand that. The latest thing that set him off was anal imagery."

"Anal imagery?" Harriet said.

"It's a big thing now in art criticism, and there's this art historian guy working on a catalogue for the retrospective, and he says the orbs and circles indicate suppressed homosexuality and something called sphincter imagery —"

"He tells Archie that?"

"He didn't tell him, but Archie got hold of something he'd written, and that caused a huge blow-up. It's happening all the time, and I have to get him chilled out and calmed down. Well, you saw him the day he attacked Lilian. He always attacks Lillian when he's upset. First he goes about the house muttering, 'That old bitch' and saying it's all her fault his life's all fucked up — sorry, Harriet — and then he works himself up into a frenzy and goes off down the street and confronts her."

"Not physically, though?"

"Well, he hasn't yet, but you never know what would happen if somebody wasn't there to stop him."

"She doesn't seem to be frightened."

"No, she doesn't *seem* to be."

"Why Lilian, anyway? Did she ever do anything to harm him, or is it just that she has the picture?"

"Oh, Harriet, it all happened ages ago. Long before I was born. He blames her because he stopped painting. I forget the details. 'There is a tide in the affairs of men,' he says, 'which taken at the full…' Well, you know the quote. Julius Caesar says it."

"Cassius, I think."

"'There's a tide in the affairs of men and some bloody woman usually fucks it up,' he says when he's on one of his rants. It's funny, really, except that it isn't funny. I mean it *would* be funny….When there were the just two of us it was OK. I could handle him. But then he found Toby."

"*Found* him? Found him where?"

"Well, downtown, I suppose. Or in the bar. I came in after work one day, and there was Archie with his easel set up, painting away, and there was Toby standing motionless the way he does. After a bit Archie stopped because I'd broken the spell or something when I came in, and they were hungry. So we sat around the table eating the leftovers I'd brought home from my cart, and Archie got a beer out of the fridge. He offered Toby one, and Toby shook his head sadly and pulled out his pockets to show he had no money and couldn't pay for anything. Well, he didn't *say* he had no money, but mimed he had no money. When you're around Toby for a bit you just fall into talking with him in this way. If he actually *says* something, everything stops as if he'd uttered a primal scream. Anyway, Archie said the beer was payment for the modelling. Then Toby let us know that if he got hold of money he tended to drink, and it was better if he stayed away from it. But Archie said a beer never hurt anybody. It was on the tip of my tongue to say it hurt *him* alright when Toby did this fantastic mime, a kind of rake's progress that ended with him sprawling on the floor. After that we had our food, and I thought he was mute, I really did. He was hungry, though, that was plain to see. He didn't need to mime anything to show that.

"A day or two later in the morning he said, 'Gotta go to work.' I nearly fainted from shock. I wanted to say, 'You can talk?' But I caught myself. It would have been so embarrassing, like commenting on a person that had lost a leg, 'Oh, you only have one leg!' So I just said, 'Work? What kind of work do you do?' Then he went and got his box and paints. I hadn't noticed his box before because he'd put it with Archie's stuff in his studio. So I watched Toby put on his whiteface, and then we walked across the park and down to the mall. He helped me wheel my cart and set it up, and then he went to the other end of the mall and went to work. So we became like partners, and we've been doing that ever since. It can be wonderful, especially on nice summer days when there's kind of a happy, friendly atmosphere down there with all the other artists. Some of them are pretty good, but it's like Toby and me, when we're going strong, we're like the king and queen of the mall."

"I know, I've seen you."

"I love my cart. Archie painted it for me with all the poppies and geraniums and put 'Carte Blanche' in fancy letters. I think that's when I became Blanche. And I take a lot of trouble with the coffee and food. It's all good stuff and delicious, though nothing that goes into it is expensive. I make avocado and bean sprout sandwiches, and everyone loves those. And crunchy peanut butter and lettuce — you'd be surprised how popular they are. And cream cheese with walnuts, and chopped egg ones with plenty of parsley from the garden. There's an art to making a good sandwich. And I'm really good at it."

"I know, I've tasted them," Harriet said.

"Anyway, after a while Archie stopped painting Toby and started looking gloomy. And Toby got down and thought he'd have to move on. And I thought it was going to end up with Archie going on a binge, and me trying to cope with it by myself. But it worked out OK. Archie said Toby could stay on as long as he wanted, and Toby turned out to be real conscientious about helping out with the house and Archie, not like some of them that just take, take, take. He'd help with the cleaning and cooking. But best of all, when Archie's in the doldrums, he'd cheer him up, because that's his work, lifting people up when they're down. So it got that the three of us settled down pretty well, and after that we didn't want anyone crashing with us, we were a kind of family.

"Toby's work is more important than mine or Archie's, though. I mean people need what he gives them. They can get muffins and coffee any place, really, but where else can they see something like Toby? Think of it, Harriet, there are all these buildings. And they're all full of people living like automatons. They don't even have their own offices. They have cubicles. Imagine spending your whole life in a box with no lid, no window, no door — just a desk with a machine on it, and a chair in front of the machine. Their entire working day is spent between one cubicle and another. They need to pee so they're allowed to go down the aisle between cubicles and sit in a cubicle just like the one they left. All modern — no chain to pull, no faucet to turn on, no towel — just an automatic flush, automatic flow of water, automatic swoosh of air to dry. If it was animals, they wouldn't allow it.

"They let them out for lunch and a breath of unconditioned air or they go to the gym and run on treadmills or peddle static bikes or lift weights. And they come down to the mall, and there's Toby. And they're mesmerized. Who knows what they see or why? Themselves or somebody else? Their present or their future? They're so stunned, they don't even know what he's saying to them. They just wonder at the technical part of it — that anybody can keep so still without twitching or blinking or itching. He puts a spell on them.

"Summer's the best time when we're both working. After the lunch hour when it's getting on for two o clock, we pack up and he helps me wheel the cart back to the shed and unload the food, and we carry the leftovers to the park and sit under the trees by the lake eating them. Then we walk the rest of the way home, and to bed, and sleep, and make love."

"It sounds like an idyll," Harriet said.

"You might think so, Harriet," Blanche said, "but it's not altogether. You see, you don't know Toby. He's like a child hanging onto my skirts. Anything goes wrong and he gets down in the mouth and sort of sulks. And, boy, can he sulk. He gets this reproachful look that you can't get away from. He wants us to go off together. But how can I do that? I can't leave Archie. They'd have him in a home. An institution-type home."

"They?"

"His children. Besides I don't want to go off with Toby. I want to be by myself, like you, Harriet. Do you mind if I keep on smoking? This is really a help talking to you like this. I'm starting to feel better."

"Good."

"You know, Harriet, I used to come up here for my music lessons when I was a little kid. It seemed like a magic place then, like going up into an enchanted tower. And Lilian was so nice. When she was young, she was like a fairy princess in a storybook. Did you ever see a picture of Lilian when she was young? Ask her to show you one sometime. She must have one, she never throws anything away. I used to wish she was my mother and I could come and live with her and have my bedroom up here and listen to all the other kids having their lessons. Now that's funny, isn't it? Can you imagine anything worse than listening to a lot of little kids playing scales and thumping out their recital pieces? 'Perkin the Rooster'? 'The Kid Next Door'? 'Fur Elise'? I played them all one time or another. We had recitals. It's not very modest to say this, Harriet, but I was the star. I was always the best. Truly."

"I believe you."

"I even played at the Centre of the Arts with the whole symphony orchestra. And in other places, too, not just here. I mean other cities — Winnipeg and Calgary and Banff. And then it all ended."

"How did it end?"

"How? Who knows? Like Archie says, 'There is a tide which taken at the full....' And sometimes it just swamps you, sweeps right over you and flings you on the sand totally wiped out. And you never really get back on your feet. Well, I should be getting back. God only knows what's happening. But thanks for letting me talk to you."

"Look, Blanche," Harriet said, "any time you want to come in here, you can, you know. The door's never locked, and if it is the key's under the mat on the top step. You can make yourself some tea or coffee, you know where everything is. And have some peace and quiet. Only open the windows if you're smoking."

Harriet didn't regret inviting Blanche to use her place as a kind of retreat. She was very sweet and grateful. But Blanche didn't want to use it as a retreat at all, at least not in the sense of having solitude and peace and quiet. What she needed was a sounding board. She wanted someone to talk to, rehearsing the events of her childhood and her past life, the ashtray meanwhile filling up with cigarette ends, which she'd discard after using one to light the next one. Harriet, sometimes exhausted from the theatre or from talking to Hope, would get a drink and sit down and not listen exactly but let Blanche's words flow over and around her.

"What I'd really really like," Blanche said one day, "is to have my own little restaurant. I'd call it Café des Artistes, and it would be gathering place for all kinds of artists — painters, and musicians, and poets. And actors, too, Harriet. And I'd put their work all over the walls. There'd be paintings and photographs and poems, and those sketches they do for costume designs in the theatre. And the food and drinks would be really cheap. And it would be like a home for the artists, and if they had no money to pay me, I'd let them have the food and drink for nothing. What do you think, Harriet?"

"It's a lovely idea," Harriet said.

"Oh, good," Blanche said, "because Archie says it's a rotten idea. He says I'd get a lot of long-time layabouts coming in for free drinks. And he says artists are better off spread out through the community and not concentrated in one place because they just starting drinking and fighting with each other."

"Archie isn't right about everything," Harriet said.

She thought ruefully how easy it was in this town to get all tangled up in other people's lives. Here was Blanche confiding her life story, and Betsey treating her as a conduit to Blanche, just as Hope treated her as a conduit to Mazo.

XV

"Stop right there!" Sandy yelled. "It's not working."
The statement rang out like the first gunshot after days of
diplomatic exchanges and a phony war, and it applied not only
to the scene in question but by implication to the entire production. They'd been rehearsing Act IV, the climactic scene
before the wedding of Mazo's daughter.

> The scene takes place in a large room full of antique fur-
> niture. The room is full of indications of wedding prepa-
> rations — there are wedding presents in boxes, some in
> the process of being unpacked. Mazo and Caroline are
> surrounded by hat boxes, and Mazo is trying on hats.

MAZO: Everything would have been differ-
               ent if we'd stayed in England.

CARO: Everything?

MAZO: Well, this wedding for one thing.

CARO: This wedding is what you're really fretting about, isn't it?

MAZO: Do you remember our plans when Antoinette first came to us?

CARO: We dreamed of a marriage to a royal duke.

MAZO: An ordinary run-of-the-mill duke would have done. Or a marquis. Or a baronet. Or even a mere knight.

CARO: We didn't ask much, but they're not exactly thick on the ground in Canada.

MAZO: Even if they were, Antoinette wouldn't have been interested.

CARO: Well, she's happy.

MAZO: Oh yes, she's happy. It takes very little to make her happy because her goals are so humdrum.

CARO: Is that why you're so downcast?

MAZO: Not just that.

CARO: If not that, then what is it?

MAZO: All my life, I've been subject to torment by weddings. They depress me horribly. If this wedding were to take place in St. Paul's Cathedral or in the chapel at Eton, I'd still be depressed. I'd still feel like an outcast from the human race.

CARO: Aha. I see. The old wound reopened. *We* were denied a wedding and you've never got over the disappointment.

MAZO: You make it sound trivial.

CARO: In view of what we've been to each other, it is trivial. Weddings mean nothing.

MAZO: That's not true. They stand for something. For public approval of a union between two people. And without that, we've been forced to live a life of secrecy and pretence.

CARO: We haven't pretended. We've been inseparable partners. Everyone knows that.

MAZO: We've pretended to be sisters, Caroline! We haven't been sisters. We've been lovers.

CARO: Hush, Mazo. The servants will hear you.

MAZO: Caroline, that's exactly what I mean. Hush, the servants will hear you! Isn't that what we've told each other all through the years? Hush, someone will hear? Why shouldn't they hear? I want everyone to know we've been lovers and not sisters all these years. I want to write it in my books.

CARO: I thought that was what Renny and Alayne were all about.

MAZO: They were. And what was that but another form of disguise. No one knew they were us. That we were them.

CARO: Fortunately.

MAZO: Not fortunately. I'm tired of playing hide-and-go-seek. Now I want to write my own story open-

ly. And it will be your story too. I
shall call it "Mazo and Caroline: A
Love Story."

(A knock at the door.)

MAZO: So, the morality squad has arrived
                   already.

CARO: Come in, Paynton.

ANTOINETTE: It's me. Are you ready for a surprise?

CARO: The day is full of them.

(Antoinette enters in full wedding regalia.)

CARO: Darling, it's a dream.

MAZO: It's a nightmare. It's hideous.

"This is supposed to be the grand climax," Sandy said, "and
all that happens is Mazo gets upset about her daughter's wedding, marches over to her desk, and decides to write frankly
about her love for Caroline. *And* the connection between those
two events is a bit tenuous."

"But what's behind the decision isn't trivial," Hope said. "It
implies something enormous. It's the outer manifestation of a
tremendous moment of revelation about her life and her work.
It's Paul's blinding vision on the road to Damascus, that kind of
thing. And after that moment nothing is ever the same. Mazo

and Caroline appear before the world as different people. Not as sisters any longer, but as lovers."

"*Implies* is the problem," Sandy said. "That's like Oedipus without the rope and the brooch, having his moment of truth and just saying he's had it up to here with married life and Thebes, he's moving out with the girls. Or abducting them to Colonus. What do you do with the rest of the play? Stage a custody battle?"

"Seems a bit of an overreaction to the wedding to me," said Beth, the artistic director.

She'd been growing more and more uneasy. She'd thought she had an ideal play on her hands, a surefire hit that had everything to satisfy the season ticket holders — the patriotic appeal of a neglected Canadian author joined with the parochial satisfaction of supporting a local playwright. That would please the Chamber of Commerce and get the Writers Guild off her back for a year. And she didn't have to worry about a lot of four-letter words in the script. Granted the plot about two maiden ladies was a bit tame, but then most of the season ticket holders were maiden ladies themselves, or at least widows who had reverted to spinsterhood. So all was well. Then halfway through rehearsals she'd found out the main characters were lesbians, and, as if that weren't bad enough, the director wanted them talking about it on stage. It was her worst nightmare come true.

"We've also got a fundamental contradiction," Sandy said. "I mean, if Mazo was so wedded — sorry — to the idea of her unsanctioned union with Caroline and her resistance to state-imposed heterosexuality, it makes no sense at all that from the start she dreamed of Antoinette making a so-called brilliant marriage."

"Too bad," said Hope, "because that's the way it was. Biographers aren't in the business of ironing out their subjects' contradictions, like scientists fixing the science to get the results the drug companies want. I have to remind you that people *are* contradictory. Full stop. Period."

"And I have to remind you that we're dealing with art, not life," Sandy said. "Creative Writing 100."

"I don't think it's so contradictory that Mazo should want a kind of social acceptance for the girl that she didn't have herself," Harriet said. "It's like risk-taking parents not wanting their children to take risks, but just wanting them to be safe. Parents are by definition conservative. In their roles as parents, anyway."

"Since when did you take such a big interest in parenting?" Hope said irritably.

"I don't think it's a contradiction, either," Beth said, hoping that all was not yet lost. "The way I see it, Mazo's a control freak who's seduced Caroline into this bizarre lifestyle. Then she tries to repeat the process by adopting another orphan and seducing her into it, too. Only it doesn't work with Antoinette, who's one hundred percent normal. So the whole edifice comes tumbling down like a pack of cards, and Mazo's left standing among the ruins. That's enough of a climax without all this other stuff."

"One hundred percent normal!" said Sandy. "I don't believe what I'm hearing. Maybe we should let Mazo hang herself. Or get attacked by killer dogs."

"This isn't Wyoming or California, it's Canada," Beth said.

"Oh right, sorry, I forgot," Sandy said. "Canada Customs stops homosexuality at the border!"

"Apart from *that*," Beth said vaguely, "the play-acting the women do is *not* normal. It's grotesque, childish, regressive, verging on the psychotic. Maybe this is the basic problem. It's ridiculous, yet this play makes it out to be romantic and wonderful."

"Ever heard of the Brontës?" Hope said.

"They were kids, weren't they? They played 'let's pretend,' the way all kids do," Beth said. "But this thing with Mazo and Caroline goes on into middle age, that's what's sick."

"Who decides what's sick and what's one hundred percent normal?" Hope said. "What about S & M and war games?"

"We're getting way off topic," said Beth.

"Not really," said Hope. "The point is that if you do a play about de Sade or Genet it's perfectly acceptable —"

"Not in this town," Sandy said. "Anyway it doesn't change the fact that what we've got on our hands is a soap opera. It lacks violence."

"Then add some violence. Have them physically abusing Antoinette. Actually they did do violence to her. Mazo was one rotten mother," said Beth.

"Bullshit. What did they do to Antoinette? They took her in and raised her. Raised her in pretty high class circumstances, when nobody wanted her. Since when did that count as a violent crime?" Hope said.

"Mazo got her and raised her to fit into the crazy play that was her life, and used her as a model for a character in her novels. That's like raising a kid so that you can harvest its bone marrow," Beth said.

"Since when was having kids ever a selfless enterprise?" Hope said. "People have always had ulterior motives for having kids — to work on the farm, to fulfil some dynastic ambition, to look after them in old age."

Brandi had been working at filing her nails and not saying much, although she was listening closely. "Look," she said at last, "I don't get a lot of this, maybe I'm too thick, but it seems to me what we're doing in this scene is outing Mazo and Caroline. Why fuck around with it? How's about a wedding in burlesque? Let them have a mock wedding or something? Nudity!"

"You've been in too many porn movies," Hope said.

"She's got a point, though," said Sandy, "the point being to present Mazo's quietly subversive behaviour in a different context."

"Antoinette comes on in this elaborate wedding dress," Brandi went on. "Let her tear it off and pass it to me. I'll strip down and put it on. That should be pretty climactic! Or will the season ticket holders have heart attacks if they see somebody without their clothes on?"

Off, off, you lendings, Harriet thought.

"We could put a notice out saying that parts of this play may be offensive to some," she said.

"The whole thing about wedding dresses is that the women are all *oohing* and *aahing* over the dress and the men are all fantasizing about its removal," said Brandi. "So there'll be something for everybody. Let me and Harriet exchange vows. Then I'll fling off the dress. Then turn out the lights. What's that opera that starts with a great orgasmic burst of music? The one with the transvestite?"

"Right. We could use the overture to *Der Rosencavalier.*"

Everyone laughed, and then quite spontaneously Harriet and Brandi moved into the scene.

MAZO: Caroline, put the dress on!

CARO: Don't be absurd, Mazo.

MAZO: Put it on, Caroline. You can get into it, can't you?

CARO: Of course I can get into it. But I'll look
         ridiculous.

MAZO: Why should you look ridiculous?

CARO: I'm over fifty years old.

(But she sees that Mazo is serious and takes off her dress.
Mazo helps her on with the wedding dress and arranges
the veil lovingly over her head. She gets a mirror and
holds it in front of her. The effect is stunning and they
both smile.)

MAZO: Paynton!

PAYN: Ma'am?

MAZO: You're a churchgoing man, aren't you?

PAYN: Yes, indeed, Ma'am. I'm a lay preacher.

MAZO: Do you have a prayer book?

PAYN: Naturally.

MAZO: Go and fetch it!

PAYN: I have it here!

MAZO: Close to your heart? (He nods.)

MAZO: Would it offend you to read the service for holy matrimony?

CARO: Miss de la Roche is working on a scene for her latest novel.

MAZO: Wrong. Miss de la Roche is working on a scene from her own life.

PAYN: Is this a rehearsal for Miss Antoinette's wedding?

CARO: You got it, Paynton!

PAYN: Then I have no objection.

MAZO: Stand before the fireplace, then. And let's begin. I'm the bridegroom.

PAYN: Dearly beloved, we are gathered together in the sight of God, and in the face of this congregation, to join together this man and this woman in holy matrimony; which is an honourable estate, instituted by God in the time of man's innocencey, signifying unto us the mystical union that is betwixt Christ and his Church...

"OK," said Hope. "How's that?"

Everyone was laughing, and on that note of general amiability, Sandy decided to call a halt to the rehearsal and to discuss it when they'd had time to think about it. So Harriet helped Brandi struggle out of the wedding dress, and they went off cheerfully.

Harriet had vaguely taken note of the fact that Ted had slipped into the theatre, as he often did when he came into town. He sat patiently watching the rehearsal in progress while he waited for her.

"Getting pretty crazy, isn't it?" she said.

"Interesting, I thought," he said.

Their steps turned automatically towards the park, as always.

"What do you suppose would have happened if we'd got married way back when?" he said.

"The alternate script," she said. "I'd have been in another city, keeping your house and kids, and you'd be down here, running around with a bit of fluff from the theatre."

"It wouldn't have been like that, Harriet," he said.

"Mazo wrote something in her autobiography," Harriet said, after a while. "'Surely there is to each of us one human being loved above all others, one house, one horse, one dog.'"

"She should have stopped with the human being," he said.

"And she should have added, it's never the one you end up with," she said.

"It would have worked for us, Harriet, if you hadn't kept disappearing on me," he said.

"When I disappeared the second time," she said, "you were married and had two kids, remember?"

XVI

Her disappearances must have seemed to him like stage exits engineered by complicated machinery — a harness lifting her into the sky or a trapdoor opening beneath her feet — because she could never bring herself to tell him what was behind them. The first time, her aunt organized everything and imposed a ban of silence; the second time was a bit more complicated.

After Harriet recovered from her father's death, she worked for a few years as a receptionist for a psychiatrist; then she got bored with that and decided to go back to school. She drifted into law because some of her friends were taking the LSATs and she went along with them. She surprised everybody — most of all herself — by getting a scholarship to law school. Her mother wasn't impressed, but Aunt Nina was so pleased she started sending her a big cheque every month for "extras."

Once classes started Harriet realized she hadn't enjoyed herself so much since the first time she went to university. Just like before, the students formed a cabal with their own private language and in-jokes. And, also just like before, she formed a bond with another student; soon they were doing everything together — sitting next to each other in class, heading to the nearest bar afterwards, studying together, and eventually living together.

The courses themselves weren't all that different from drama. She'd watched a lot of television during her years in the workforce, and she'd concluded that the best contemporary drama happened in the courtroom. It had all the elements of great tragedy — heroic characters, conflict, great dialogue, and big moral issues. She could see that when she eventually got into the courtroom it would be just like theatre. Meanwhile she enjoyed the textbooks, which reinforced that conclusion. She relished the dialogues in the criminology textbook and thought the passages of comic relief equalled the gravediggers in *Hamlet* and the porter in *Macbeth*. She and Joel read them aloud to each other to break up the monotony of studying:

> CLERK: Do you swear that the evidence you shall give touching the matters in question shall be the truth, the whole truth, and nothing but the truth so help you God?

> WITNESS: Fuck it, man. I ain't testifying.

> JUDGE: I'm sorry, I didn't hear you.

> WITNESS: I ain't testifying, man. Fucking charge me. Whatever you fucking want, man. I ain't testifying.

JUDGE: I find you guilty of contempt in the face of this Court.

WITNESS: Up yours, you dick.

JUDGE: And I sentence you to a period of incarceration of six months consecutive to any —

WITNESS: Fuck you, you goof.

JUDGE: — time now being served.

WITNESS: Goof.

JUDGE: Get him out of here.

WITNESS: Fucking goof.

Harriet didn't tell her aunt that she and Joel had moved in together; she just said she had a friend over.

"You seem to have him over quite a lot," her aunt said, after he answered the phone three times in a row.

"Yes, well, we're dating, and we study together in the evenings," Harriet said.

"Well, just be careful," her aunt said. "You don't want anything happening this time around."

But what happened this time around had nothing to do with being careful. It blew up unexpectedly out of a case she read aloud to him about a photographer, who turned up at a wedding so drunk that he could hardly stand up. All the wedding photographs were out of focus, so the bridal couple sued for expenses to stage the wedding all over again. It was complicated by the fact that guests had flown in from all around the world.

"Talking of getting drunk …," Joel said, and he went to the fridge and brought back two beers.

"I think big weddings are stupid anyway," said Harriet. "Let's never have a big wedding."

"A wedding, big or small, isn't in the cards for us, Harriet," Joel said.

"It isn't?" she said, puzzled, wondering if he had a wife he hadn't told her about.

"Well, I'm Jewish," he said. "You know that." Of course she knew it. He had a yarmulke in the drawer and went to the synagogue on the High Holidays, and there had been a nasty incident involving a friend who asked him to be his best man but withdrew the invitation because his father, a prominent judge, objected to a Jewish best man. Also Joel went home to Shabbes dinner every Friday; he never took her along, saying she'd find it boring. She accepted the explanation because she never took him with her when she went home for Sunday dinner. But she never thought it would affect their relationship; she didn't think Jews went in for arranged marriages like Muslims. It came as a complete surprise that he couldn't marry a Gentile; if he did, it would kill the old grandmother.

They weren't exactly star-crossed lovers; she really didn't want to get married. She'd just made an offhand remark, but having it laid out on the table like that changed the balance of the relationship, and she began to feel he was taking advantage of her. The upshot was that they started quarrelling and he moved out of the apartment. It was a big upheaval just before exams at the end of the first year, and once he was gone she lost interest in studying. Not only that, but she didn't feel comfortable on campus, because she didn't want to run into him with a new girlfriend. She started wandering around the parks all day and didn't even turn up for her finals.

The dean of the law school was sympathetic and understood what had happened without having to be told all the details. She said she'd help her reschedule the exams or do her courses over again if she wanted to. But Harriet had lost interest in school altogether, so playing Portia in *The Merchant of Venice* was the closest she ever came to being a lawyer. Her mother, who thought it was a crazy idea all along, was pleased she'd dropped out of law school. The one who was devastated was Aunt Nina.

"You didn't get pregnant again, did you?" she asked bluntly.

"No, I did not," said Harriet.

"I bet it had something to do with that guy," her aunt said, and slammed down the phone. They'd had an up-and-down relationship for years, and after that it fizzled out. Around the time she quit law school, Harriet heard that Mrs. Herbert died, and then a few months later her aunt died of a heart attack. Harriet didn't bother to go to Vancouver with her mother to the funeral.

"I didn't know she had a bad heart," Harriet said when she saw her mother afterwards.

"Me neither," her mother said. "Maybe it was the shock of finding out he had no intention of marrying her whether he was free or not. He probably never had."

Then her mother told her that Nina had left her car and all her belongings to her, and all her money to Harriet. She'd written a nasty letter after Harriet dropped out of school and the monthly cheques had stopped, so Harriet was sure that leaving her all that money must have been an accident. She'd probably been so spun round with Mrs. Herbert dying that she'd never got around to changing the will. Harriet said she felt as if she'd stolen it or got it under false pretenses, and she didn't think she could bring herself to spend it.

"Oh, you'll bring yourself to spend it alright," her mother said, "and if you can't you can pass some of it along to Donna. She and the kids can use a bit of help."

Harriet decided to keep it.

It amounted to a tidy sum, and so Harriet didn't rush to find a job, and that left her plenty of time for brooding. It also left her plenty of time for drinking, and she could now afford more than beer. It was at this time that she developed her taste for good whiskies.

She was doing her usual run to the liquor store one day when she bumped into Ted. He'd been in the U.S. doing graduate work in engineering for the last three years, but he looked just the same. The main difference was that he was now wearing a gold band on his left hand; he'd acquired a wife as well as a degree while he was away. He said his wife was pregnant with their second child, and they were "having a difficult time of it." He was getting involved with the theatre and doing stage lighting again.

"Why don't you get back into it?" he said. "I think you'd like this Little Theatre group I belong to. We're doing *Macbeth* next, and they're trying out for parts."

"Oh, sure. I could be one of the three weird sisters," she said.

She'd got pretty sloppy since she broke up with Joel, and she knew she looked like a wreck. But after she went home, poured herself a stiff one, and turned on the television, she remembered that time she'd seen the play in Vancouver. It seemed a big coincidence that of the whole Shakespearean repertoire they should be doing that same play now in Saskatoon. She thought it must be an omen, and she went to try out for Lady Macbeth. What happened was exactly what she'd said in jest; she ended up playing one of the witches. "Typecasting," she said, looking at herself in the mirror.

It was a small part, but she started to feel better. Going to rehearsals gave her a routine, and the play gave her something to think about apart from her messed-up life. She read it over and over, and soon she memorized everyone else's lines. And she started seeing a lot of Ted again. At first he walked her back to the apartment after rehearsals, then he started coming up for a drink, and before long it was "off, off, you lendings" again. She told him about Joel, and he told her about his wife. He'd felt out of place on the big Ivy League campus, and marriage had fended off the loneliness. It wasn't working so well since they'd been back in Saskatoon.

The next thing that happened was that the woman playing Lady Macbeth dropped out. Harriet knew all the lines and was ready to step into the part.

"What happened?" she asked the director. "Did she get pregnant?"

"Nah," he said, "she was just too unstable and hysterical."

"Oh," Harriet said, "unstable and hysterical."

It was a huge relief to the director to find someone who already knew the lines, and he agreed it was a neat idea to have one of the witches play Lady Macbeth. He wished he'd thought of it himself. He wasn't so keen on Harriet's other idea — that Lady Macbeth should be pregnant and her gentlewoman should be a midwife. He said there was absolutely no evidence for that in the script, and he vetoed the suggestion.

"You're not having a baby, are you?" he said.

At first she was disappointed at having her interpretation rejected, and then she decided that it didn't matter whether he went along with it or not, because he didn't have to know. She could play the part in her own mind just as she liked. And that's what she did. It was her first experience of building up a character psychologically, creating for that character a rich interior world, full of complexity and conflict but curiously inaccessible to the audience.

The reviews in the local papers singled her out for rapturous praise, raving about the way her performance ricocheted between tenderness and savagery. They used words like "nuanced," "chiaroscuro," and "perfectly calibrated." Most of them used the word "maternal," and several said it was hard to account for the source of power in her performance.

Ted was genuinely pleased by the praise and said he couldn't understand why she'd stayed away from the theatre for so long. She couldn't, either. It seemed to her, as she looked back over her life, that up to that moment it had been a series of missteps. The one single thing that had happened to her that really should have happened and truly belonged to her was that she saw a performance of *Macbeth* in Vancouver when she was nineteen years old. That play and the one in Saskatoon connected, all the non-essentials that had happened between them fell away, and at last she'd learned what her destiny was.

She also learned some other lessons. One was that having a sense of direction doesn't eliminate some very untidy detours and digressions in the future. It's possible only in retrospect to see which has been the road ahead and which has been the road to nowhere.

Another lesson she learned at the same time was that safe sex isn't as safe as it's cracked up to be; she should have been on the pill. Eventually she surfaced in Vancouver, playing the lead role in *Anthony and Cleopatra*. But before she got there she made another long and painful detour. She knew she couldn't face what she went through the last time she got pregnant. This time she carried it to full term and then gave it up for adoption. It was time-consuming, painful, and expensive, but she managed to make her own arrangements and get through it without involving anyone else. She also followed the advice her aunt Nina had given her the first time around and didn't tell Ted. She didn't need his help because she had her inheritance. A huge chunk of it went on her disappearing act and its aftermath.

XVII

Harriet set off one afternoon towards Hope's house. Hope had not attended any rehearsals since the clash over Act VI, and they all assumed she was in seclusion, rewriting it. Harriet's fervent wish was that the sudden summons, transmitted by phone through Lilian, meant that Hope had finished the scene and wanted to use Harriet as a sounding board for the revision. Her dread was that Hope would press her for yet another description of the meeting between her aunt and Roger Herbert. In preparation for this eventuality, she tried to think of diversionary tactics as she walked along the road. Perhaps she could raise another topic.

"You can't buy a baby!"

"That's what you think!"

"But who could you buy one from?"

"From some damn fool who doesn't have enough sense to know what she's doing."

Had her aunt meant that Mazo had literally bought the baby? And if so, how had she spent the money? Had it been funnelled into the big cars, the apartment, or had it been shunned as blood money? The thought occurred to her — not for the first time, but always with the same feeling of revulsion — that perhaps her aunt had banked the money and earmarked it for Harriet, hoping she could get the education her aunt had missed out on. She wondered as she made her way over to Hope's house if her legacy had been blood money from the sale of her aunt's child.

In the timeless world of the theatre, the days of the week lost their demarcations, but the fact that it was Saturday soon announced itself in a cacophony of car horns drifting over from the main thoroughfares. Weddings! Summer Saturdays were crammed with them, a whole year's worth of weddings being squeezed into the warm months in order to avoid the hazards of a winter wedding — the bride and bridesmaids shivering, anxiety about the pastor's ability to get to the church on time, out-of-town guests stranded. So the weekends of July and August were frantic with last-minute dashes to the altar.

Small parks dotted the city, wooden signs bearing the names of the service clubs that established them — Rotarians, Lions, Elks, Whelks, and Kiwanis. Their original purpose was to provide small areas of green space for recreation amid the highways and strip malls, but they had all willy-nilly become monuments to human procreation. On Saturdays they were taken over by bridal parties to serve as the backdrops for wedding photographs. The bridal pair would be transfixed forever against a background of trees, a small waterfall, or a gazebo, evoking an illusory Garden of Eden; the camera's selectivity excluded the chaos just beyond the picture frame — the racket of passing traffic, the stench of gasoline fumes, scorched tires, and Kentucky Fried Chicken, the assembly line of other bridal pairs jostling for their turn in front of the waterfall. On weekdays, the garbage was cleared away by city workers, and the parks regained a vague semblance of peacefulness. Then they became the province of young mothers, burdened with baby buggies and toddlers — the results of ceremonies staged there some years earlier.

Harriet paused in Rotary Park to watch one couple being cajoled by a photographer out of their sullen trance into a pantomime of faked happiness. It was an uphill battle; the bridal party was elegant, the bridesmaids in sweet pea colours, with balls of pink and purple flowers suspended by velvet ribbons from their gloved wrists. Harriet guessed the occasion had been ruined by weeks of internecine strive, family rivalries, cost overruns, and squabbles about the guest list. The photographer seemed to be sober, but his efforts to redeem the situation were hopeless.

"Hey, this is a wedding, not a funeral!" he tried. Then someone called out an obscenity, got a laugh, and *click*, the situation was saved. This moment, this summer afternoon, this waterfall, this corner of a small prairie city was preserved forever in celluloid.

Harriet walked on, her spirits unreasonably lowered by the tawdriness, the falsity, the conveyor belt of couples lining up at the waterfall. She felt for the pair — even sulking, they looked pleasant enough — nudged into marriage by family custom, the expectations of friends, false hopes, or who knows what. She found herself wishing them luck, hoping the picture would end up being shown to grandchildren and not dismissed as "my first husband, what a jerk," or "my first wife, what a bitch!"

Hope was in the front garden when Harriet arrived, and her greeting was drowned out by a sustained trumpeting from the horn of a passing car festooned with white and pink pompoms.

"Committing matrimony seems to be a noisy business," Hope said. "Makes you feel like the Ancient Mariner, doesn't it?"

Harriet didn't smile.

"What's wrong?" Hope said.

"Look, Hope," she said irritably, "I've said all I can about that meeting between my aunt and Mazo's cousin. D'you mind if we don't go into that today?"

"You *are* in a bad mood," Hope said. "You need a drink to cheer you up. I've got a surprise for you. I've added an extra scene to the play, and you'll be the first to see it."

"*Another* scene?" said Harriet, relieved. "They'll have a fit."

And so they went through to the garden, where chairs and a table were arranged under the apple trees that flourished there in spite of Hope's refusal, on ideological grounds, to look after them or eat their fruit. Sitting down, Harriet picked up the script from the glass tabletop and began to read.

As she read, Hope stayed close to her side, watching her face and fussing with bottles and ice cubes, while the wedding horns went on honking all over the city. It occurred to Harriet that Hope was unusually agitated about the new scene, and it was not long before the reason for that agitation became clear.

Vale House in Windsor. In the drawing room, the two women have been interrupted in the midst of their afternoon tea by the announcement of a guest.

MAZO: Back so soon, Roger. Pleasure again or business this time?

ROG: Neither. There's a problem with the kid.

MAZO: I won't take a defective child.

ROG: It's not going to be defective.

MAZO: Is it going to arrive prematurely?

ROG: There will be two children. Twins.

MAZO: Well.... Nature has a way of playing some very odd tricks on all of us, but this is highly unexpected.

ROG: You said at the beginning that you'd hoped for two children.

MAZO: That was at the beginning. We finally agreed on one child. That's what I'll take.

CARO: One nursery, one nanny would do for two as well as one. What difference would it make?

MAZO: It makes a difference to me. We struck a bargain for one child to be delivered, Roger. You can't back out now. I want one child at the appointed time. Everything has been arranged as we planned it three months ago — our return to Canada, our soujourn in Italy, all our tracks covered. The secrecy is as important to us as it is to you. It can't be changed now.

ROG: But separating twins. It seems unnecessarily cruel. To them and to the mother, who already feels —

MAZO: Under the circumstances, a certain amount of discomfort for the mother is inevitable. We've discussed all that. There's to be no sentimentality, no future contact, no messiness. You undertook to ... cope ... with the mother and provide for her future.

ROG: But I didn't anticipate this latest development, and I'm damned if I know what to do.

MAZO: For someone of your resourcefulness and immense power, that's hard to believe.

ROG: These affairs with women are so confoundedly complicated.

MAZO: You'll simply have to turn to an agency.

ROG: Absolutely not. No agencies. No records.

MAZO: Then obviously you must make another private arrangement. I wish very much that you hadn't disturbed us with all this, Roger. It's very distracting and I trust it is not a precedent for the future. The plans remain as they were — we come to Toronto, Caroline travels west with the nurse, your people deliver the child to the train. Now I shall go and rest. You seem to forget that it's my writing that must support this child. I can't have the circumstances of my work disturbed.

(She stalks out, but reappears in the door-way.) Stay for dinner, if you wish, Roger. But I don't want to hear anything further about this matter.

ROG: Hell of a mess for me.

CARO: Yes, I'm sorry.

ROG: Surely you have some influence. Can't you get her to change her mind?

CARO: Oh, no. She never does. Not when she's made it up like this. It's done.

ROG: I don't understand. Is it obstinacy, malice, or mischief?

CARO: None of those. It's very complicated. It all has to do with her imagination and her writing.

ROG: I don't get it!

CARO: Her life feeds her writing. Already she's been creating scenes in her next novel — the birth of a child, the writing for a child. Preparations have been going on for weeks.

ROG: So she said.

CARO: No, I don't mean *my* preparations, I mean the preparations of the fictional family. She's been writing feverishly.

ROG: Good God, it must be complicated. Like living a double life.

CARO: No more complicated than your double life, I shouldn't think. You'll simply have to make another arrangement for the twin. Surely that's not impossible?

ROG: No, it's not impossible, but it's damned untidy, and I don't like a mess.

CARO: So you have had a fall-back plan all along?

ROG: I didn't want to use it.

CARO: Am I allowed to ask what it is?

ROG: You always did like to have secrets to keep from her, didn't you, Caroline? Is that why you...?

CARO: That was over a long time ago, Roger. It never happened. But secrets, yes, I do.

ROG: I wonder why.

CARO: You shouldn't. You've just seen how much

power she has. Over all of us. And you've
seen how she wields it. Having secrets is the
only way I know of undermining her
absolute control over me. So tell me what
you intend to do. Your secret will be safe
with me.

ROG: I'll have to get help from the kid's mother.
She has a sister...

CARO: Well then, the perfect arrangement!

ROG: No, not perfect. Much too close for comfort. And the sister already has a family of
her own. And they're ... well ... they're
farmers of some kind. On the prairies.

CARO: Farmers on the prairies? My! Strange kind
of pride you have, Rog, to care whether or
not your bastard child is raised in the afflu-
ent circumstances to which you yourself
are accustomed.

ROG: I'm not a monster, Caroline. I do have
some feeling for the poor little brat. I don't
like to think of it raised in poverty, suffer-
ing deprivation.

CARO: Come, Roger, it's just as likely to have a
happy life as the other one — the out-
doors, animals, fresh food.... Isn't country

life supposed to be healthy? A loving family, a normal family, brothers and sisters.

ROG: One sister, I believe. The father drives a cab
in the winter.

CARO: A farmer, the driver of a cabriolet! Both
honest occupations.

ROG: Not funny, Caroline. Sometimes I think the
two of you are a pair of heartless brutes.

Harriet set the script aside, feeling as if her head were in a
bubble, surrounded by a great and unnatural silence. For a
moment she thought that what she'd read had induced some
strange mental state. Then she realized what the silence was. The
wedding racket had stopped. The bridal parties had moved
indoors and gone underground.

All around the city, in church basements and recreation
rooms, knives and forks were clattering and glasses were being
raised in toasts. Spoons were being tapped against cups to cause
the victims to kiss each other one more tedious time for the
entertainment of the onlookers. Harriet wondered if the gloomy
couple had cheered up, reconciled to their fate, and already
decided between themselves to make the best of it. Hope was
coming out of the house carrying a tray, with an unusually anxious expression on her face.

"Why didn't you just come out with it and tell me?"
Harriet said.

"Because I wasn't completely sure of it myself," Hope said.
"It all remained in the realm of speculation until I met you."

"And when did you enter this realm of speculation?"

"A few months ago, when I stumbled on the fact that you and Antoinette share a birthday," Hope said.

"Then you didn't need me," Harriet said. "That fact told you everything you needed to know."

"Facts never tell you everything you need to know, Harriet."

XVIII

Engrossed as she was in her own past, it was little wonder that Harriet, criss-crossing the mall on her way to and from rehearsals, was oblivious to the storm that was gathering there. If she sensed any change in the atmosphere, she simply put it down to the increasing heat of the dog days of August. And when Blanche told her that Toby was getting stressed out, she thought she was referring to the intense concentration required by his work.

The trouble started innocently enough when one day some kids, restless and fidgety themselves, begrudged the mime's calm immobility and began heckling him.

"Hey, clown," they yelled, "there's a yellow jacket crawling up your leg. There's a bug going in your ear. A big black one. A hornet."

Their shouts caused a few heads to turn, necks to crane backwards, jaws momentarily to stop chewing. Previously the crowd, taking their cue from the mime's absolute immobility, had been subdued, but now their interest was piqued. They stirred a little, some giggled softly, waiting expectantly to see if the mime would relinquish his act and show signs of human frailty.

The mime remained perfectly still as always. He was a slight, boyish figure, standing on a box, all in black save for the white circle of his face and his white-gloved hands. On his head he wore a Greek fisherman's hat. His arms stretched forward in front of him, one hand raised slightly above the other, like a clockwork toy waiting for a child to turn the key and set it in montion.

Soon the cries became more insulting, first with the inevitable sexual innuendo, then with explicit charges of homo-sexuality, pedophilia, and bestiality. Graphic details were added, for the kids' undeveloped imaginations had been supplemented by filth snatched from the open sewer of the Internet. At this, the crowd perked up, grew more alert. No one shouted "Knock it off, kids," or "Go take your Ritalin," although one or two stomped off in disgust. A woman, dragging a toddler by the hand, said you couldn't go anywhere these days without hearing four-letter words. Still the mime remained unmoved, his arms outstretched, and his unblinking gaze fixed above the crowd.

Then the hecklers, incensed by his lack of response, became more aggressive. Their taunts became more daring, their lan-guage more obscene. But nothing, it seemed, could penetrate the mime's trance, not even so much as to cause the flutter of an eyelid. Enraged by their impotence, the kids brought in rein-forcements. They recruited older, meaner kids for whom play-ground bullying and animal torture were not mere pastimes, but vocations. These were specialists who understood the impor-tance of timing — how to space assaults on their victims so that they relaxed and were doubly jolted when the attacks resumed.

The specialists also brought out the instruments of their trade, simple props at first — paper darts that didn't make much of an impact, balloons that exploded, causing those close to them to jump. The mime himself, such noisemakers constituting a basic part of his training, remained unaffected by them. His stoicism earned a flicker of admiration here and there, but this was lost in the growing excitement of the majority, and it served to fan the rage of the tormentors, who were working themselves up into a frenzy.

The battle was now engaged in earnest; the phony war had ended, and the real war had begun. The escalating skirmishes made the workers hurry from their desks at the strike of noon, fearful of missing any part of the unfolding drama. A break in the weather — a rainy spell or a brief shower — might have eased the tension, but the heat wave lasted, and the sun beat down relentlessly.

In subsequent days the assailants brought on the heavy artillery — rubber bands, slingshots, catapults, and peashooters. The first time the weaponry appeared, the spectators' excitement rose to a new level, only to be followed by a temporary setback. The rubber bands failed to reach their target, landing randomly in the crowd. The anticlimax produced a wave of annoyance. But the next day the momentum was regained; the peashooters were more precise, the projectiles bouncing off their target and bringing a smattering of applause from the crowd.

It was the slingshots and catapults that were the most effective, for they were loaded with lethal projectiles. A pebble grazed an ear, and a piece of granite aimed at the mime's cheek landed dangerously close to his right eye. A small bead of blood appeared and trickled slowly down the mime's cheek. At the sight of blood, the crowd swallowed, drew a collective breath, and became absolutely still. The spectacle was now reaching its climax. The mime clearly had two choices: he must either admit defeat by stepping down from his box or be immolated by the volley of missiles. There was a long moment of suspense.

It was during this moment that the mime acted. For he too was a master of timing. When he sprang into action, his movement was so quick and deft that it took the crowd completely by surprise. They remained rooted to the spot, their reflexes frozen, unaware of what was befalling them. It was only after the brown shower had rained down on their heads that they realized what it was, broke ranks, and scattered, howling and screeching.

The assailants, from their positions on the periphery of the throng, were naturally unscathed. Nor did they linger to savour their triumph on site, but, fearing some kind of official reprisal, fled the scene even before the police materialized, pausing on their flight down the mall only to overturn the sandwich cart, sending it with all its contents crashing to the pavement.

It was onto this scene of chaos that Harriet emerged from the cool depths of the theatre. She sniffed something foul, saw that the buskers and pavement artists had disappeared and that the crowd, in the state of excitement induced by a catastrophe, had fragmented into small groups. The pavement was strewn with garbage, several police officers were talking to people, and journalists were moving among them with cameras on their shoulders and recording equipment in their hands.

"What happened?" she asked.

"It's the clown," a woman told her, "they've arrested him."

"Toby?" said Harriet. "What for?"

"He went crazy. He started throwing shit at everybody."

"Throwing shit...," said Harriet, looking at the scattered cups and sandwich wrappings.

"No, *shit*," the woman insisted, "you know, *shit*! His own shit."

"My god!" said Harriet, noticing what seemed to be dog turds among the debris and connecting it for the first time with the stench that filled the air.

"What the fuck's goin' on?" asked Brandi, who had left the theatre with Hope a few minutes after Harriet.

"It's Toby," Harriet said. "He seems to have lost it. They say he started lobbing pieces of shit around."

There was no lack of documentation, for punditry had set in quickly, and a group soon gathered around them.

"The cops took him off in a van. That girl of his, too."

"They had to take her, he's a deaf-mute."

"That clown had a real mean look about him."

"He used to hang around our barns until the men kicked him off the place. Crazy about horses. Used to say he wanted to be a jockey."

"He musta been kicked in the head."

"He needs kicking in the head. Her too."

"He was stoned. She pushes drugs from that cart of hers. I seen that with my own eyes. Bringing it out in bags like it was candy."

"Yeah, them poppies all over it tell you something."

"Well, she'll have to find another place for peddling it from now on."

Harriet, Brandi, and Hope, glancing up the mall and noticing the wreckage of the cart for the first time, automatically moved towards it. It had been thrown over with such force that one of the wheels had come off and rolled away and the other was badly buckled. The side panels with their beautiful flowers were intact, but the canopy and the wooden poles that supported it were smashed to pieces. The coffee urn had rolled quite a distance, and there were sandwiches and pieces of fruit everywhere.

"What do you think we should do?" Harriet asked.

"I've got the truck. If we can drag this over to the road, I'll bring it around," Brandi said. They picked up the dented coffee urn and put it on top of the cart with all the broken bits of canopy and wood. They managed to stick the wheel back onto the axle, and then they dragged the whole thing precariously over to the road. A lot of people threw hostile glances in their direction, but no one offered to help.

"Fuckin' asswipes," Brandi said.

"Where do we go with it?" Harriet asked, after it was loaded onto the back of the truck.

"I guess you'd better take it over to Archie's place," Hope said. "He'll help you unload it, and I'll go round to the police station and see if there's anything I can do there."

After they'd pounded on Archie's door for a good ten minutes, they peered in the windows, and, seeing no sign of life, started carrying some pieces around to the back of the house. They were just wondering what to do about the cart, when the back door opened. It was Archie, yawning and stretching as if he'd just got out of bed. He said he'd help, but he needed a cigarette first, so they went inside and sat at the kitchen table while he had a beer and dry-looking piece of leftover pizza.

"Breakfast of champions," he said. "Want some?"

He listened without surprise to their account of what had happened on the mall.

"Lot of this performance stuff around these days," he said morosely. "Used to be galleries just had pictures on the wall and a bunch of jackasses gawking at 'em. Ran into a guy in the bar the other night. 'I'm a performance artist,' he says. 'I stage happenings.' Looked like it'd be a happening if he ever got off his ass."

"Toby wasn't doing performance art," Harriet said. "It was unpremeditated."

"Yeah, that's what this jerk told me," Archie said. "It's spontaneous. We don't plan it, it just happens."

"He was fuckin' goaded into it," Brandi said. "A bunch of kids pestering him with water pistols."

"Well, he should've pissed on them while he was at it," Archie said. "Will he do time?"

"More likely a fine," Harriet said. "I think people will help him raise the money. They'll probably charge him with gross indecency."

"I've seen stuff a helluva lot more gross than that," Archie said, "back in the good old days. Kleinholz. Jesus Christ. What a guy! They have these volunteers at the gallery. Docents, they called themselves. You shoulda seen their face. Hey, either of you gals interested in buying a picture? I can give you a good price."

After they got the cart unloaded, Brandi seemed disinclined to drive back home, so Harriet asked her in for another drink, hoping, as they walked down the street, that Lilian would be occupied by something so she wouldn't have to introduce her to Brandi. But even as she stepped into the hallway, Lilian called out, as if she'd been waiting for Harriet's return.

"Is that you, Harriet? I suppose you've heard about the to-do on the mall," she said. "I've been apprehensive for days about something untoward happening down there. I simply don't believe what's happening to this town. Something should have been done long ago about those ruffians who hang about the downtown area with nothing better to do than annoy people. This'll be just the pretext needed to clear the mall and kill everything that makes it alive and vibrant. They've been just waiting for something like this, and he's played right into their hands."

"You mean Toby?" Harriet said. Lilian didn't answer. She had just noticed Brandi standing behind Harriet, in the doorway.

"If that's you, Brandon, you may as well step inside rather than lurking in the hallway," she said.

"Good afternoon, Miss Lilian," Brandi said.

"I told you not to call me that," Lilian said. "You make me sound like the mother of some jumped-up peanut grower."

"Sorry, Lilian," Brandi said. "I pick it up from Mum."

"And how is your mother?" Lilian said. "These must be very trying times for her."

"Yes they are," Brandi said, "but she was very pleased to get your card."

"It must be a great relief to her that you've come home and settled down," Lilian said.

Brandi looked at the carpet. "Would you like some eggs?" she said at last. "I can give them to Harriet at the theatre and she can bring them home to you."

"Are the chickens laying well?" Lilian asked

"Pretty well," Brandi said. "We always have a few dozen on hand."

"A dozen would do very well," Lilian said. "Harriet couldn't carry more than that. Brown."

"I know," Brandi said, "brown, fresh, free-range, large size."

"Do you still practise your instrument?" Lilian asked.

"I gave it up for the guitar," Brandi said.

"Hmm," Lilian said, "not one of those electrical things, I trust."

"Is there anything we can get for you, Lilian?" Harriet asked, when no one had spoken for a while.

"Not at the moment," Lilian said. "I'm very angry and confused just now. Disappointed, too. Perhaps more disappointed than angry. Perhaps more confused than anything else." They left her trying to get the right balance between the three adjectives that defined her state of mind.

"Whew!" said Brandi, when they got upstairs. She had undergone a total personality change while talking to Lilian, and now she was sweating, as if she'd just executed a daring escape.

"Were you a student of hers?" Harriet asked.

"Please don't ever ask me about that, Harriet," Brandi said. "Just give me a drink."

"Another beer?" said Harriet.

"Something stronger, if you have it?" Brandi said.

XIX

Lilian's prediction proved correct. The repercussions of the incident on the mall were enormous, and they spread with every passing day. Wildly improbable rumours circulated, fanned by callers to radio talk shows and by letters to the editor. In one version, Toby (generally referred to as "the clown") was gay, and had provoked the attack by making a pass at a bystander; in another he and his girlfriend were pushing drugs (the overturned cart had revealed the stash), and he had gone berserk as the result of an overdose.

Mrs. Pike was highly indignant. She asked Harriet if she had heard what that beggar did in the mall. Harriet replied that he wasn't a beggar, he was an artist, and Mrs. Pike looked as if that explained everything. One of her neighbours had been passing through the mall and had got a brand new jacket ruined.

"She burned it in the back yard. Now she's worried she might be HIV positive," Mrs. Pike said.

Blanche, unconcerned about the destruction of her cart, fretted that Toby would spend the rest of his life in jail.

"It's not a capital offense," Harriet said. "He'll probably get a fine or a short sentence at most."

"Harriet, you don't understand," Blanche said. "It's not what he did, it's what he'll do in court. He won't act the way you're supposed to do, and he'll get charged with contempt. He'll go mute and not answer questions. If they ask him if he regrets his action, he'll say no."

Lilian busily clipped the articles out of the paper and started a new file on the subject. She was also trying to compose her own letter to the editor. She appealed to Harriet for help. She said she wanted to talk about puritanical forces that disapprove of spontaneity and innovation and try to push creativity and inventiveness into the realm of the obscene, so that those who most benefit mankind get pilloried.

"I think you ought to say 'humankind,'" Harriet said.

"Thank you, Harriet," Lilian said. "I know I'm old-fashioned. It's the way I was raised. I don't speak the way young people do. But by the same token, their words are often offensive to me, and that's part of what I'm trying to say. When disrespect is encoded in the language, it needs to be pointed out and excoriated. That's precisely what my letter's about."

"Do you mean that Toby was disrespectful or that the kids who baited him were?" Harriet asked.

"Both were reprehensible," Lilian said. "I have no doubt that Toby was provoked, but Archie's been a bad influence on him. He sets a very poor example of self-control and self-discipline. However, that's not the only thing I'm protesting. I very much disapprove of the word they keep using when they speak of what he did. They shouldn't give currency to it. I can't bring myself to say what that word is."

"I see what you're getting at," said Harriet, at last. "It's been around a long time. I think Chaucer uses it. But, Lilian, I'm not sure that this, you know, deserves a letter to the editor."

"Harriet," Lilian said with a sigh, "you don't understand."

Hope kept talking about the history of mime, how it was the oldest form of dramatic expression, and how beginning with Plato it was associated with indecency. Harriet assumed that Hope intended to use Toby's plight as grist for classroom discussion, but she learned that Hope, in fact, was the one person who was being constructively helpful in defending Toby. She had immediately got in touch with a former student who had gone to law school. Hope and the lawyer were casting around for the best person to appear as an expert witness, if one were needed to vouch for mime as a time-honoured art form. Harriet offered her services and was offended when they told her the expert witness had to be someone of irreproachable respectability. They placated her by explaining that it couldn't be anyone associated with the theatre; it had to be a CEO or a clergyman.

The prospect of Toby appearing in court made them all nervous. They tried to persuade him to plead guilty, but they feared he would ignore the lawyer's instructions and complicate everything by changing his plea to not guilty at the last moment. These fears proved groundless, as he understood that the legal procedure was just another performance. When the judge asked him if he felt remorse for the harm he caused, the entire courtroom watched in silence as he assumed a posture of abject shame and penitence. No words were necessary, nobody laughed, and the judge seemed quite satisfied. Hope quickly found an anonymous supporter willing to pay the fine.

Although Toby looked entirely different without his makeup and could have gone about the town unrecognized,

Blanche insisted on assembling a disguise for him. This was a literal military camouflage, which she acquired from the Army & Navy Store, consisting of battle fatigues — baggy pants and a matching jacket in shades of green and beige. Toby was so delighted with it that he dyed his hair blonde, got a brushcut, bought a pair of granny glasses, and became a born-again skinhead. He also perfected a belligerent way of walking and embarked on a new life, apparently unaware of the forces of madness he had unleashed.

It was a relief for Harriet to escape from all this insanity into the calm of rehearsals. It became clear to her, however, that the theatre was not a hermetic entity, sealed off from the outer world. One morning Beth convened a meeting and spoke to the assembled cast and backstage workers.

"I'm sure I don't have to tell you what's going on around us at this time," she said. "Even those of you who don't stoop to reading the local papers will have heard about the ordinances presently in city council to get the buskers and street people removed from the mall and to cancel the gay pride parade. There's a lot of support for both these ordinances, and in the current climate I'm concerned that some of the scenes in the play might be offensive to the season ticket holders."

"If I hear another word about the goddamn season ticket holders I'm leaving town," Sandy said.

"Lucky you that you have that option," Beth said. "For most of the people in this room, the theatre's our bread and butter. It's survival, and ours depends on the regular subscribers."

"Fuck the regular subscribers," Brandi said, *sotto voce*.

"We have a situation at the moment in which anything even mildly pornographic is liable to stir up a hornets' nest."

"The play isn't mildly pornographic," Sandy said.

"I'm talking about the relationship between the two main characters," Beth said, "and the fact that it's gotten more and more sexual. When I read the original script, it wasn't sexual. At least not overtly. Quite frankly I wouldn't have touched it with a ten-foot pole if it had been. I didn't anticipate the turn it's taken. It's been getting more and more risqué every time we go through it."

"What are you suggesting?" Hope said.

"What I'm suggesting is that we go back to the original script so anyone can interpret the relationship between the women as a friendship between cousins. The audience won't stand for a couple of lesbians feeling each other up all over the place. We could have a mass walkout, especially at the matinees, which are popular with the blue rinse crowd. So cut out all that stuff. It's easy to do, and it will spare us a lot of grief. Not to mention sparing us the need to defend ourselves and explain what we're doing."

"I agree," said a voice from the back of the room. "I think there's something weird about outing these two women who didn't want to be outed. Didn't Hope say one time that Mazo said her hobby was privacy? I think we should respect that. We owe them that much."

It was Greg, the young actor who played Speaks in the first scene. Harriet wondered if he so identified with the part that his own personality was submerged. That happened sometimes with young actors playing small parts.

"It's precisely at a time like this, with homophobia on the rise, that we need to take a stand and refuse to suppress the erotic dimension in the relationship," Sandy said, ignoring Speaks. "By doing so, we make the play relevant to the moment. That's what theatre's supposed to do."

"This isn't agitprop. And this isn't New York or Paris," Beth said. "We're working in a small prairie town, and this is a struggling provincial theatre. Of which I happen to be the administrator, and in which role I have the final say."

"But I have rights, too, as a playwright, and my rights include not letting my play be eviscerated," Hope said. "It's a question of artistic integrity and censorship. I could appeal to the arts board and the writers' organization on that. I'm sure their support would counteract the negative reaction of the season ticket holders."

"I wouldn't count on that," Beth said. "This theatre happens to be the only professional outlet available to most of them, and they won't be eager to cut themselves off from it over some moral issue. Besides, who's talking about eviscerating the play? I thought it was supposed to focus on a neglected Canadian writer and get people reading her again! Instead, we're letting that get drowned out by making it about this love affair between the women. That's gotten blown out of all proportion. And, like Greg said, there's something nasty about outing them when all they craved in life was their privacy."

"There are two things to be said on this subject," Hope said. "It's true that Mazo said that privacy was her hobby. Actually she said that privacy was her obsession. That was a public statement telling people to leave her alone. But when I read her works, I sense another voice running throughout, one that's muted but very insistent all the same. And this is the voice of a bird in a cage, saying, 'I can't get out! I can't get out!' All that bird imagery is a way of telling us how much she craves freedom. Being private isn't freedom if it means being hidden away in a closet and pretending you're something you're not. One part of her needed to hide for fear of scorn. Another part of her yearned to be let out. And that's the creative tension that informs all her work. What the play can do is let her out. And we aren't dragging her out of the closet and holding her up to ridicule. We're doing it respectfully — even though some of the audience, no doubt, will sneer and snigger. That's one thing. The other thing is your remark that suppressing the real nature of their love for each other will spare us the need to defend what we're doing. My intention from the start was to provoke discussion, and I relish the opportunity to explain and defend."

"Needless to say, I'm with Hope one hundred percent on that," Sandy said. A chorus of voices murmured, "Me too."

"Couldn't we compromise?" Greg said. "Perhaps Brandi and Harriet could tone down the touchy-feely bits for the matinees."

"It's not that simple," said Beth. "The audiences aren't homogeneous. The matinees don't consist entirely of old ladies, and a lot of the season ticket holders go to the evening performances. What I might do, though, is send out a notice warning that the play may offend some sensibilities. I could offer rain checks to those who want to skip this performance and give them an extra ticket to another performance of their choice."

"It's a rotten idea, but it just might boost attendance," Sandy said.

"And spark debate," Hope said.

"Perhaps I can work something out along those lines," Beth said.

"We can go ahead, then, as is, for the dress rehearsal?" Harriet said.

"Right," said Beth.

So the crisis was defused, though no one felt particularly good about the outcome.

"Wasn't Hope terrific?" said Harriet as she walked with Sandy along the mall, now denuded of its colour and music.

"Oh, very eloquent," said Sandy. "Best peroration I've heard since Oscar's 'the love that dare not speak its name.' By the way, Harriet, your landlady's pretty eloquent, too."

"My landlady?" Harriet said. "You mean Lilian?"

"The very same," said Sandy. "Great letter in the today's paper. You didn't write it for her, by any chance, did you, Harriet?"

"Of course not," Harriet said. "What's it about?"

"Well, she starts out with Thomas Crapper, whose creativity and ingenuity resulted in one of the world's great inventions — the flush toilet. And what did he get by way of a reward? He got his name made into a dirty word. She compares him with Alfred Nobel, the inventor of dynamite, and all his ill-gotten gain. And she manages to twist them into an attack on the city fathers who, on the pretext of guarding our morals, and under the dubious banner of family values, have banished art and music and fun. So now the mall is as drab and dreary as the central square under a totalitarian regime."

"Oh," said Harriet, "crap. I didn't understand."

XX

There was a full house for the dress rehearsal, at which the tickets were half price. Harriet caught glimpses of several familiar faces in the audience, and when she walked into the wine bar in the upper foyer after the show, she realized that Hope's drama class was there en masse. Typically, Hope had made a project out of the rehearsal. She was holding forth at the far end of the foyer, the students grouped around her, some sitting on the floor. They were engaged in an animated discussion, and once Harriet had got hold of some wine and struggled free of the people who wanted to chat with her, she gravitated curiously towards them. They smiled at her in a shy and friendly way, and she saw that most of them were holding scripts that were heavily annotated and highlighted. They were analyzing the scene in which Mazo and Caroline decide to adopt two children.

CARO: (Suddenly suspicious.) Mazo, what's back of all the reminiscence and recrimination this evening? You aren't getting restless again, are you?

MAZO: I'm always restless.

CARO: Oh, Mazo, don't be restless again. It's perfect here — you've said so every day.

MAZO: It is. It's the very perfection that makes me anxious. I worry that it might slip away and out of my grasp. I don't want our lives to turn sour here. Perhaps we should make a change while everything is perfect.

CARO: But we've moved so often and nothing has suited us so well as this old rectory with its ivy-covered walls and towers. You said that your imagination thrives here, and that even driving back to the house after an outing inspires you.

MAZO: It does, it does.

CARO: Well then?

MAZO: Well then.

CARO: You can't want to move to another baronial manor, can you?

MAZO: We've lived in Devon, in London, in

Windsor, in the Cotswolds and back in Devon again. There's nowhere else in England that I care to move to.

CARO: It's Ireland then, isn't it? You've taken it into your head to move to Ireland where the Roaches and the Whiteoaks have family roots? I always thought that might be in the cards.

MAZO: Well, it isn't in the cards. At least not now.

CARO: That's a relief. It's a terribly damp climate. (Then suddenly struck by a thought.) You're not thinking of ... not Canada, Mazo?

MAZO: Caroline, my imagination needs Canada. I bit into that apple just now, and do you know what I saw? I saw a sunlit stretch of land beside Lake Ontario, glowing under an Indian summer sky. I saw the flame of reddening maples and the glimmering pallor of silver birches. And I saw Jalna. Caroline, Jalna is in Canada.

CARO: Jalna is wherever we are. Jalna was on an ocean liner in mid-Atlantic once. Jalna was in Palermo. It was in a *pensione* in Florence.

MAZO: But the life of Jalna has to be fed by our daily life.

CARO: And nothing but Canada will do?

MAZO: It isn't just Canada. It's Canada and something else.

CARO: Something else?

MAZO: I want a child.

CARO: Oh, you want a child.

(There's a long pause while Caroline contemplates the implications of this statement. Finally she seems to come to terms with it, to grasp it. She rises, walks around the table to Mazo's chair, stands behind it, and places one hand on Mazo's shoulders. There is faint, very faint Jalna music, but it is somewhat halting and uncertain. Then she speaks.)

CARO: Renny, when Rags drove me into town today, it wasn't, as I told you, in order for me to buy a hat. It was something else. I had an appointment to see the doctor. Renny, there's something I have to tell you....

MAZO: Oh, Caroline, do sit down. Yes, there'll be children at Jalna, a whole generation of them. Renny and Alayne will have children. Finch and Sarah will have children. Piers and Pheasant will have children. There'll be children all over the place. But before they do, I want us to have a child.

CARO: (Shrugs, sits down, and becomes practical again.) I should point out that you are well beyond child-bearing age. And I trust you don't expect me to bear you a child? There are limits to what the imagination can produce, even one as lively as yours.

MAZO: Do you remember when I so badly wanted us to be married?

CARO: Well, we couldn't be married. In some things we just have to settle for second best, for not having what other people have. We could only adopt each other as sisters — Oh, adopt! Now I see. You want to adopt a child!

MAZO: There's no reason why we shouldn't.

CARO: Two single women in late middle age aren't very acceptable to the adoption agencies, you know.

MAZO: With my connections, it could be arranged. The publishers can't afford to relinquish their hold on the Jalna books, and the Macmillans have influence everywhere. I've already spoken to Harold.

CARO: Your fondness for travel would have to be curtailed for a start. As would a lot of other things — weeks in town during the theatre season…

MAZO: Nonsense, you've seen the way people travel with children. They take along nurses and nannies. All the English people do that. Children wouldn't affect our lives any more than we wanted them to. We wouldn't need to see them any more than we wished. The servants could take care of them. You know how the English do. They see them in the drawing room for an hour after tea when the children are cleaned up.

CARO: What a lot of trouble for one hour a day.

MAZO: It wouldn't be one hour a day. Not for us. I'm just saying that we need not necessarily change our way of life. It will all be managed as smoothly as possible. We'll close up this place, spend six months travelling in Canada, and then we'll sail back to England. When we get back here we shall be a complete family, and no one will be any the wiser.

CARO: And when we have this child —

MAZO: Children, Caroline. There will be two children. A boy and a girl.

CARO: You have this all planned, don't you?

MAZO: Oh, Caroline, can't you imagine it? Two children and we can give them simply everything. They can have everything we lacked. We can redeem our childhood through them. They can grow up in beautiful surroundings attended by devoted servants, elegantly dressed, cared for. There'll be no ailing mother, no endless chores for her or shabby clothes for him. No feckless father, no cramped little sitting room full of foul-smelling uncles, no squalid meals. We'll put his name down for Eton, and hers for ... well, wherever they send the girls. A finishing school in Switzerland — I'll ask Lady Dorothy. He can perhaps be a guardsman, a diplomat, and who knows, in the fullness of time, perhaps a member of the House of Lords. She can be a debutante, be presented at court, and in the fullness of time, marry a viscount or a marquis. Can't you see us at the wedding? At the ducal home? Surrounded by a bevy of titled grandchildren — Lady Arabella, the Hon. Felicity, Lord Rupert....

CARO: Already I'm beginning to imagine it. Arranging the coming-out balls, arriving at St. Margaret's for the wedding. Oh, Mazo. What a splendid idea. It's one of the best ideas you've ever had. Suddenly the Whiteoaks begin to seem like a very provincial lot indeed.

MAZO: Don't be such a snob, Caroline. Don't forget the Whiteoaks made everything possible.

CARO: Of course, Mazo. Without them we'd be nothing.

MAZO: Nothing.

"Hey, don't let me interrupt," Harriet said, because her arrival on the fringe of the group seemed to have stopped the discussion.

"We were talking about the echoes," one of them said. It was the student called Bitha who had pressed Harriet to compare Bernhardt and Mazo when she'd visited the class.

"Echoes?" said Harriet.

"The echo of that earlier scene where they invent the French marquis. You know, the guillotined ancestor. We think he broods over the whole play like the ghost of Hamlet's father in *Hamlet*."

"He can't brood over the whole play because he isn't even mentioned until the middle," Jason said. He was now quite awake and holding a tattered copy of the script.

"That's true," said Bitha, "but when he is finally mentioned, he seems part of something, the culmination, really, because there've been like all these images leading up to the mention of him."

"Oh yeah, like what images?'

"Well, the first thing the audience sees is the portrait of Mazo, but it's just a head, so it looks like a severed head, almost a Medusa figure —"

"That's reading way too much into it."

"Then there's the dialogue about the person in the portrait. Her books supported the publishing house, but her own story is erased. 'There is no story.' So the whole play starts with that contradiction — these works by a person whose whole life is shrouded in silence. It's all about disembodied voices and the silencing of certain voices. There's that scene where Mazo becomes famous overnight and reporters are clamouring to talk to her — so she gets visible, and at the same time she loses her voice. Then the beheaded ancestor is introduced, and he's a Huguenot. If ever a group was silenced, it was those Huguenots."

"The audience isn't going to know about Huguenots," Jason said. "I'm taking history and I had to look them up. The audience needs more pointers, and these details need explaining."

"But the images of decapitation, amputation, and silencing have been running throughout. There's this subtext, but to bring it to the foreground would ruin it," Bitha said.

"If I hear one more word about silenced voices I think I'm going to throw up," Jason said.

"I agree with Bitha," another woman in the group said, completely ignoring him. "Some of the audience will get the subtext and some won't. It's sort of like Jesus and the disciples. 'Lord why do you speak to us in parables?' 'So those that get it, will get it, and those that are clueless won't.'"

"But it isn't like they're reading the play," Jason said. "It goes pretty fast, and the innuendoes get lost."

"I don't think the subtext gets lost," said Bitha. "There's this whole business of aristocrats throughout. The aristocratic Bostonians that Speaks is an authority on. The Masseys in Toronto. It's clear that measured against them the women have no legitimacy. They're relegated to the margins, their claims to aristocratic pedigree as make-believe as their play. Then they get their revenge. They somehow pull themselves up, or try to, into the genuine aristocracy. So their ambition to link Antoinette to the bloodline of some English ducal family is perfectly understandable."

"Say, does the publisher have to be called Speaks?" Jason said. "The only one who thinks he has the right to speak for them. Isn't that a bit too obvious?"

The discussion raged on, with the students showing no signs of tiring, until the bar was being packed up and Hope said they'd continue the discussion in class the next day. As usual, Hope offered Harriet a ride home and circled around by Fortescue Street on her way back to the crescents.

"Are Bitha and Jason both drama majors?" Harriet asked.

"Bitha is," Hope said. "Jason, I believe, is planning to be a lawyer."

"They remind me of when I was a student and I felt passionate about the interpretation of plays," Harriet said. "I can see why you like teaching."

"This is a particularly good class," Hope said, "the kind that comes along once in a blue moon. Most of them are like a bunch of french fries. You had a lot to do with this one, Harriet. Your talk was like a shot in the arm. They've been fascinated by the play ever since you spoke to them."

"So if nothing else comes of the play, it's been a great teaching tool."

"Don't talk like that, Harriet. The play'll be a great success."

"Come up for a drink?" Harriet said.

"Heavens, I had four glasses of wine already," Hope said. "I shouldn't even be driving. Get a good night's sleep, Harriet."

And so Harriet went in alone, closing the door as quietly as possible because it was late and Lilian would already be asleep. She'd had four glasses of wine too, but wine never did it for her, and she intended to have a good glass of whisky before turning in for the night.

As soon as she entered the apartment she picked up a trace of perfume and, following it, found a vase on the kitchen table containing several stems of white freesia and maiden-hair fern. Beside it was a bottle of white wine. There was no card, and the idea of someone, no matter how well-intentioned, coming in while she was away made her feel uneasy. She put the bottle in the fridge, noting as she did so that it was chilled and ready to drink. When she opened the cupboard above the sink where she kept her bottles of hard liquor, she saw that they had all been removed.

As she drank the wine, she tried to think of when Hope had arrived at the theatre. It seemed she'd been there when Harriet walked in, but then she could have driven by the house after Harriet left and still have arrived at the theatre ahead of her. But then, the wine wouldn't have stayed chilled for so many hours. And the vase of flowers was out of character. But Hope was devious and could have left it for that reason. Or could it have been Blanche or Archie who had simply run out of liquor and borrowed hers? That she could easily check by asking Blanche, who would fess up without hesitation. "Oh, Harriet, I'm *so* sorry...." Somehow Harriet was sure Hope was behind all this, because she was the only one who had a stake in how much Harriet drank and if she woke up with a murderous hangover.

Harriet lay in bed, unable to sleep for hours without a proper nightcap and with the students' discussion and Bitha's remarks going round and round in her mind.

XXI

As the rehearsals gathered momentum in the days before opening night, Harriet felt more than the usual dread. It wasn't just that the end of the play would be in sight, but also the end of so much else. And once again she'd be cast adrift like a passenger with no specific destination at the end of an ocean voyage.

Hope was sanguine about Harriet's future and elaborated constantly on the good life she could have if she stayed on in the city.

"There are always sessional jobs in the department," she said. "You'd have a whole class of Bithas."

"But you said yourself that was a rare class."

"That's true. For me, it was. But you'd be different. A big part of teaching is theatre, and you're a natural at it. You brought the class together."

"No, Hope. It was your play and the way you got them involved in it."

"Well, you'd have parts in lots of plays, and that would feed into your teaching. There'd be a waiting list of students wanting to get into your classes. You'd be a star."

"I can't imagine anything more pathetic than being a local celebrity in a town this size," Harriet said. "I'd end up pandering to everyone's idea of an artist, flouncing around town in costumes that get more eccentric every year, emoting at readings in bars, my habits becoming the stuff of legend. I could wind up like Archie."

Already Hope was in the grip of one of her brilliant ideas. She had a tin "Brilliant Idea Box" full of them written out neatly on three-by-five cards. Her latest one was for a one-woman show with Harriet in the star role, touring all the small towns and big cities of the prairies. Harriet would perform extracts from some of the great Shakespearean female parts. Or Hope could adapt passages from Virginia Woolf, the Brontës, George Eliot. She was brimming with ideas.

"'You can never imagine,'" she quoted, "'what it is to have a man's force of genius in you, and yet to suffer the slavery of being a girl. To have a pattern cut out — "this is the Jewish woman; this is what you must be; this is what you are wanted for; a woman's heart must be of such a size and no larger, else it must be pressed small like Chinese feet; her happiness made as cakes are, by a fixed receipt…"'" Oh, Harriet!"

She constantly suggested titles: *Thinking Back Through Our Mothers, Women in Love, Mothers and Daughters.*

"Or do you think something snappy like *Top Girls* or *Women on Top*?"

It would be scripted by Hope, and Harriet would, once again, become a project of Hope's. And eventually she might even end up in living in the flat at the top of Hope's house. Harriet could imagine the invitation being offered any day now: *It would be so convenient, Harriet, and I know all your guilty secrets by now.*

Not all, Harriet thought, *not all, by any means.*

Ted said much the same as Hope, the phrase "you could

have a good life here" on both their lips. He could help her to buy a place of her own on one of the tree-lined streets in the old neighbourhood that she liked. She'd have her freedom all week and a husband on weekends, or the other way around.

"The best of both worlds," he said.

The worst of both worlds, Harriet thought.

It wasn't the prospect of making a future with Ted that caused apprehension there. It was something else: she'd known from the first moment they met again that eventually she would have to tell him about the child. Ever since their reunion, she'd been rehearsing what she thought of as a confession, trying to make it sound reasonable.

"There's something I have to tell you. Remember years ago when I played Lady Macbeth? And then I disappeared? Well, I had a baby. We had a baby."

"Why didn't you tell me?"

"Because I was afraid."

"Afraid of what, Harriet?"

And there was something else from her past crying out to be exorcised. Ever since the Saturday of the weddings, when she'd read the new scene, Harriet had known she had to make a journey to meet someone. With Hope's help, of course. Hope had already composed a letter of introduction and worked out the itinerary.

"There'll be plenty of time to decide your future," Hope said. "We can think of it when you get back from your trip."

"What was it like?"

"It was a she. A girl with red hair."

"It's easy now to trace adopted children."

"She could trace us. If she wanted to."

Against all reason, she thought about Bitha, who was the same age.

"What kind of a family does Bitha come from?" she asked Hope.

"Farmers, I think," Hope said. "Why do you ask?"

"I wondered if they were theatre people," Harriet said.

One day the director, who had overheard Hope talking about her plans for the one-woman show and the sessional lecturer positions, took Harriet aside.

"You'd be crazy to stay here," Sandy said. "It would be a terrible mistake. The parts would dry up and you'd be stuck. You're too good for this place. Look, I really like working with you, Harriet. Come down to New Mexico, to Angel Fire, to the theatre in Santa Fe. It's hot right now. You'd love the place, and you'd fit right in."

"New Mexico, Santa Fe, Angel Fire," Harriet said, repeating the talismanic names, as if they offered an escape. "It sounds marvellous."

"We do tons of exciting experimental stuff. Our next project's unrehearsed Shakespeare. Acted out spontaneously, without rehearsals, and with the audience visible to the actors. Just like the Elizabethan companies did it."

"They did?"

"Sure they did. There was no time for rehearsals. They did a new play every week, a different one every day, and the actors were given cue sheets instead of scripts. All this endless rehearsing and perfecting and blocking of scenes has built up over time. And something's lost in the process. It's time to scrape it away and get back to essentials."

Harriet made a mental note to check this out with Hope.

"Generally it doesn't work unless we use young actors unfamiliar with the Shakespearean repertoire, but you have such a rotten memory, Harriet, you'd do just fine. Think about it."

All these thoughts swirled in Harriet's mind and added to the stress she felt in the run up to the first performance. But the accumulated stress paled compared to the shock of learning just before curtain time that Brandi had disappeared. She'd been driving back and forth to the farm every day, tearing along the back roads in her battered old truck, always exceeding the speed limits. The entire group gathered backstage, most of them making ineffective suggestions about calling the hospitals or calling the police and asking each other when they'd last seen her. Hope was catatonic, and Beth said she'd known all along that something like this would happen. Sandy, the only one who remained unruffled, got hold of Bitha, who knew the script by heart, and started giving her instructions. They were just fitting her into her costume when Brandi walked in.

"He croaked," she said.

"Oh, Brandi, I'm so sorry," Harriet said.

"Well, don't be, he was a mean old bastard," Brandi said, but Harriet noticed that her hands were shaking.

So amid all the pandemonium, and twenty minutes late, the play opened. And once again *le trac* hit, just as Harriet had feared it would. Only it didn't take its usual form — a great roaring in her ears followed by a silence and paralysis. The scripted words disappeared as before, but this time others leapt from somewhere into the space where they had been. She was beginning to see that her memory lapses were not random, but the result of speaking lines that caused a shock at some deep level of her consciousness. This time it happened when Mazo brought up the subject of adopting a child.

"To lose one parent is a misfortune," Harriet said, the words from another script jumping to her lips, "but to lose two parents, to lose two parents…"

"Oh, Mazo, don't be restless again," said Brandi, now fully in control of herself. "It's so perfect here — you've said so every day."

"The closest of all human bonds," Harriet persisted, "is that between two women, biologically identical, united from the moment of conception … but all the forces in the world conspire to tear them apart. And mostly they succeed. Some remain together, but more often they are wrenched from each other's arms, like loved ones torn apart by war. Refugees and displaced persons, they wander in the wilderness. Sometimes, having taken up arms on different sides, they face each other across gullies and ravines, and fail to recognize each other. Some stumble into each other in strange places…"

Brandi made several valiant efforts to get the dialogue back on track, but eventually played along until Harriet, in her own time, came back from wherever she'd wandered off to and re-entered the script as it was written. Then they proceeded without incident to the end of the scene.

"Hope must have been shitting bricks," Brandi whispered as they left the stage.

In fact, Hope was astonishingly accepting of Harriet's extemporizing. Harriet was learning that, like most obsessive types, once one obsession had run its course, she quickly turned to the next one. Ever since the afternoon of the weddings, both her enthusiasm for Harriet's memories and for transforming those memories into dramatic form seemed to have been waning.

"That monologue you suddenly embarked on," Hope said. "It might be the best thing we salvage from this play. We could use it in the one-woman show."

It was the first inkling Hope had given that she had any reservations about her play. And so Harriet repeated the monologue in subsequent performances, elaborating on it as she went along.

Ted, faithfully, and without apparent boredom, came to every performance on both weekends he was in town. During the second weekend, Harriet decided it was time to tell Ted about the baby. After the show, instead of going to the hotel, she asked him back to the apartment. Although they had to creep inside quietly, his visit lacked the trappings of a romantic assignation. Ted, as he always did in new surroundings, reverted to type and went about inspecting the construction of the place. He tapped the walls and noted where one wall had been removed to make a larger room, another built to make the kitchen.

"So this is where you've been hanging out?" he said. "And what's up this staircase?"

She'd known when she rehearsed this scene in her mind that when he walked into her bedroom he would examine its construction before he gave her his full attention. He went ahead of her up the narrow staircase and saw the dumpsters he'd heard about. It wasn't the paintings that interested him, but the frames, and how they were hung. Swinging one aside, he revealed what she'd never suspected — a small door with a latch opening into a crawl space.

The space was full of boxes, each one sealed, labelled, and dated — correspondence, newspaper clippings, archival material, sheet music, old vinyl records. Without realizing it, she'd been sleeping night after night surrounded by the paraphernalia of Lilian's entire life. One small cigar box, labelled "photographs," seemed to have been opened recently, for it lacked the layer of dust that covered the other boxes.

Together they pulled it out, flicked open the lid, and, sitting side by side on the bed, began looking at the photographic record of Lilian's life. There was Lilian at about eight years old in a little wicker chair in the garden in front of a row of hollyhocks; Lilian with a kitten; Lilian playing the piano; more photographs of Lilian playing the piano; Lilian in a long satin gown in an artificial pose arranged by a professional photographer; Lilian with a group of young musicians; Lilian with Archie standing by her side…

Harriet pulled it out and held it to the light. At first she thought they were dressed up for a costume ball. They were both barefoot and fair-haired, Lilian's long and loose, falling in tendrils over her shoulders, a perfect picture of *jeunesse dorée*. Archie was wearing a white shirt with full sleeves, open at the neck, and Lilian, also in white, was in a dress that looked like a Mexican…

That's exactly what it was — a wedding dress — and this was a wedding photo. It had been taken in a small chapel that could have been anywhere in rural Saskatchewan, except that the dark-skinned minister and the plain altar behind them suggested Mexico or Cuba. It was a picture of pure, innocent joy, stalled in time. As Harriet looked at Lilian, Blanche's words came back to her: "When she was young, she was like a fairy princess in a storybook." There *was* something of the fairy tale about them, both smiling, as if they were playing a game of "let's pretend."

"So your landlady isn't a vestal virgin after all," Ted said.

It was true. But how had it happened? Had they eloped in order to escape the round of bridal showers and rehearsal dinners? And who was the person holding the camera that caught this moment of hope and happiness in a snapshot? How long had the idyll lasted, and how had it ended? Not amicably, Harriet was sure of that. She looked at it for a long time, and still held onto it when Ted closed up the box.

It suddenly seemed ominous, as if it cast a shadow over their own future together. Ted sensed it too, and they lay down to sleep without making love. Harriet had forgotten that she meant to tell him about the child. The moment had passed, and the family life he led elsewhere was left to go on undisturbed by it, and unruffled.

XXII

There was no question of renting a wreck, even if one had been available at the Victoria airport, because she was far too intimidated by Antoinette. She imagined her sister against the backdrop depicted in the photograph albums she had seen long ago — the mansions in various countries, the yachts, the stables full of ponies, the exclusive schools. She felt she had to arrive in style, at least in as much style as she could muster at short notice and with her limited funds. And so she went to one of the expensive car rental booths.

The conversation over the telephone had been all about directions, how to get from here to there, driving north from Victoria over Malahat Mountain. "Just shoot straight up the Island Highway," Antoinette said. "It hugs the coastline most of the way, then when you come to the first set of traffic lights, there's a huge sign. You can't miss it." Harriet had tuned out after the first set of lights, knowing that she could ask directions along the route.

"The country road will bring you directly here," Antoinette said. "Come here for a drink and then we'll have lunch at the clubhouse. Tell them to call me when you arrive at the security booth."

"Security booth? It's not a military base, is it?" said Harriet.

"No, no. It's a gated community. Unauthorized persons aren't allowed inside, but I'll call your name down to the booth and they'll let you in and tell you how to get to the house from there."

"Thanks," Harriet said. "I'm looking forward to meeting you."

"Yes, me too."

It was a curious place. She joined a row of cars lined up at the security booth, and when her turn came she gave her name and Antoinette's. They waved her through immediately, instructing her to take a right turn here and hang a left there. Once inside she found herself in a small park that resembled the set for a historical movie. There was a stream with a rustic bridge over it leading to a duck pond, at one end of which stood a large water wheel. This apparently was intended to be decorative, since it was immobile and lacked the machinery necessary to make it function. Not far away, a small herd of deer was nibbling at the grass. The atmosphere of quaint rusticity was marred, however, by the anachronistic costumes of the people trailing about the park. They all seemed to be golfers, in carts and on foot, in pairs and foursomes, all wearing sporting outfits in pastel shades.

Harriet followed the road between rows of vinyl-sided and stucco houses, which were painted in the same pastel shades as the golfers and had a disconcerting uniformity, as if they had been mass-produced for a vast game of Lego. Each one was surrounded by a small garden, planted with shrubs so neatly trimmed that they might have been plastic. The road curved, and in the small spaces between the houses Harriet caught glimpses of a stretch of water with mountains on the other side. At the end of the row, a woman stood in the garden waiting, while a white poodle sniffed around the paths.

"Antoinette?" Harriet said, leaning out of the window.

"Toni'll do," the woman said.

Harriet was nervous, and the full absurdity of the situation struck her only in retrospect, when Hope was conducting one of her usual catechisms. She wanted to know just how it felt to come face to face with a long-lost double. She was thinking of writing something on the subject. "A lot of literary journals are wanting to run special issues on the theme of cloning or the new fertility technology," she explained.

"So what did you do after that?" Hope said.

"Well, she directed me to put my car in the driveway. Parking was not permitted on the road. Then she picked up the poodle and introduced me to it. And we talked about the poodle. It was called Pinky. Her friend had one from the same litter called Pansy. There was a law about having only one dog per house."

"A law?" Hope said.

"Well, a rule. They have all these rules and regulations."

"And then?"

"Then we went inside, and there was a lot of business about fixing drinks, and how we liked our drinks, and so on. There was this really spectacular view outside the picture window, and so I admired that. And she pointed out various landmarks. Salt Spring Island. Deep Cove. The airport. Then the phone rang, and she said, 'I can't. I have a visitor, I told you.' It was someone wanting her to make up a four for bridge. 'I don't know,' she said, 'I haven't asked.' Then she asked if I played bridge, and I said I didn't and that I would have to push off after lunch because I had a hotel reservation. I sensed she was hugely relieved that I wouldn't be hanging around for the rest of the day. When that was all settled, it was time to go to lunch. The whole thing was stage-managed so there wouldn't be any embarrassing confidences or intimacy.

"Of course, it was strategic to plan lunch in a public place with so many distractions. Perhaps because I'm in the theatre she was afraid of something theatrical, unwelcome hugs and kisses, being held at arm's length while I exclaimed, 'Let me look at you!'

"The young waiter at the clubhouse obviously knew her because he produced 'the usual' before she asked. 'The usual' was a double martini with two olives. Her manner towards him was very flirtatious. I began to see that was a habit she had, cozying up to anything in pants, as we used to say."

"Did she have too much to drink?"

"I guess she did. She'd fortified herself with a stiff one before we left the house. Anyway. 'Is this your sister?' he said. 'I could tell she was, just from looking at the both of you. Alike as two peas.' 'And can you tell which is the younger one?' Toni said, coyly. 'Nah. Wouldn't want to do that. Cause a family feud,' he said."

"Was there a resemblance?" Hope asked.

"Oh, I think she'd told him her sister was coming out for a visit," Harriet said.

They were the same height, their faces the same shape, but Toni's makeup was as heavy as stage makeup, her dark hair dyed blonde, big earrings, painted nails, flashy rings, lots of gold chains, and quite heavy in a soft and pudgy way. Harriet beside her felt mousey with her dark graying hair, cut blunt and casual, her face naked of lipstick, rouge, eyeliner. But she was slimmer, had a good figure still, and could wear tight pants and a tight turtle neck, and she walked with the grace of someone trained for the stage. She definitely looked the younger of the two. What could they have told him?

We're twins, separated at birth, adopted into totally different fami-
lies, meeting today for the first time — for what? To compare lives? And
at the behest of one of us only. One having pressed for this meeting, the
other nervously enduring it. Wishing she'd never agreed to this in the
first place, longing for it to be over so she could escape into the imper-
sonality of the bridge table. "I bid two hearts."

"How did the play go?" Toni asked conversationally, filling
in the gap while they waited for the food to appear.

"Good houses, good audiences, and the reviews were
mixed," Harriet said modestly. There was no point going into
the nature of the mix. The play had been panned, but her performance had been praised as brilliant.

"The local paper usually sends a sports reporter who finds
all the plays boring. But there happened to be a big Toronto crit-
ic in town for an opening at the art gallery...."

She waited for Toni to ask what he said, but no more questions were forthcoming.

"Would you have liked to see the play?" Harriet asked,
intending the question as an icebreaker.

"No," said Toni. "I gave up seeing plays a long time ago.
Don't even watch them on television."

"When did you discover you were adopted?" said Harriet,
deciding on a direct approach.

"I always knew. Everyone did. It was obvious." She took a
long draught of the martini.

"I found out much later. It was a shock," Harriet said.

"Must have been," Toni said. "Mind you, I didn't find out the
circumstances of my adoption till much later. That was after
Mazo was dead and I was getting a divorce. I had a confronta-
tion with my aunt."

"And she told you?"

"I wouldn't exactly put it that way. She didn't want to tell me anything. I'd say I pried a few facts out of her. Not all, by any means."

"Not all?"

"She certainly wasn't going to tell me who my parents were. I think she'd promised Mazo not to, and those promises were sacrosanct. She probably thought Mazo would come back from the grave and haunt her, if she did."

"So how did you find out more?" Harriet asked.

"My lawyer dug it all out. How about you?"

"It was the woman who wrote the play. She'd researched Mazo's life pretty thoroughly, and she needed me to confirm her speculations."

"Oh, yes. Joy somebody. She got in touch with me. A nosy old thing, asked a lot of questions, which I refused to answer. It was none of her damn business, and besides, she seemed to know more about my life than I did," Toni said.

"But she did tell you some things you didn't know?"

"Tried to," Toni said. "She tried to conduct me on a guided tour of my childhood. Look, Harriet, I put all this behind me a long time ago. I really have no interest in it *at all*. As I told you about the play, I haven't the slightest interest. I live in the real world now. My whole childhood was a play. They were playing at being English aristocrats. I was playing the beautiful heiress, destined for a so-called brilliant marriage. Only it didn't work out, unfortunately. For them, that is."

"It didn't?" said Harriet.

"Right from the start, it didn't. I was a normal kid, and I liked doing normal things. I liked sports, being off with my friends. And they had this fantastic life planned out. I spent most of my life acting a part in somebody else's play. When I got married I played the society hostess, working on charity balls, entertaining. I was what they call in the newspapers a 'socialite,' whatever that is. So I got out of that."

"But you knew him? Our father?"

"I still have trouble with that name," Toni said. "He was Uncle Roger. He always brought good presents. But then there were a lot of uncles that brought good presents. The only thing that was different about him was that he always brought pictures of his sons. For a long time, I thought I was supposed to marry one of them. Anyway, he seemed to think I was hugely interested in his sons."

"That's what I remember, too," Harriet said.

"I thought you never knew him," Toni said.

"I met him once, briefly. Our mother and father together. Only I didn't know they were my mother and father."

"Weird," Toni said.

"He talked about his sons then, too, how I should meet them one day. It pissed off my aunt ... my mother ... and they had a kind of a row."

"Maybe he had a fantasy about gathering us all together, his sons and his wild oats," Toni said. "They were older than us."

"Did you want to meet them?" Harriet said.

"Not in the slightest. Did you?"

"No, it was you I wanted to meet," Harriet said. "From the first moment I saw your photos I was fascinated by you. I even stole some pictures of you, and I read the Jalna books to find you in them."

"Well, you were looking in the right place there," Toni said. She pushed her plate away and drank some of the fresh martini that had materialized beside it.

"They had this gardener–chauffeur with them for years in England and Canada, and he had a son. We grew up together like brother and sister. Well, not quite like brother and sister. When I was seventeen I got pregnant. This was a huge upheaval in their lives. All their plans and schemes suddenly gone haywire! Of course, they hadn't a clue what to do. They must have panicked and called Roger, and he must have said, 'Send her out to Vancouver and I'll get it taken care of.' So I went. Or was shipped off, rather. I was terrified. His secretary met me at the station and arranged everything. No sign of him the whole time. I thought she was very weird. Well, I was such a snob then. It was the way I was brought up.

"I stayed in her pokey little apartment that looked out over English Bay. You could smell other people's cooking in the hall and hear them through the walls and ceiling. Well, there was a sign of him, actually. She gave me her bedroom, a small room with the best view. I got so bored in there by myself that I went through her drawers. She had taken a framed photograph of him off the dresser and put it in the drawer. As soon as I saw it, I put two and two together. I knew she was his mistress. There were some pictures of me, and some pictures of her with another kid who was her niece. I guess I didn't really put two and two together, did I?

"She tried to be nice to me, to comfort me. I saw that later. She told me she'd been in the same mess herself one time.

"'Oh, what did you do?' I asked.

"'Carried it to full term,' she told me, 'and then an adoption was arranged.'

"I asked her if her family made her do that, and she said, no, it wasn't her family that made her. So I knew it was him. She said she'd spent most of the nine months in a little cottage by the sea, and it was a happy time and only the ending was terrible. I asked her how it could be happy, and she said it was happy because all along she thought she was going to keep the kid. She said what I was doing was the best way. All this stuff came back to me when I found out she was my mother. Pretty weird, eh?"

"I wonder what was going through her mind when she told you all that," Harriet said. From the expression on her face, Harriet gathered that Toni wasn't in the habit of wondering what went on in other people's minds, so she changed the subject.

"Do you ever see the father of your child?" Harriet asked. "I mean the chauffeur's boy?"

"Oh, yes. Years later — it was at Mother's, that is, Mazo's, funeral — he turned up, and we started seeing a bit of each other. He's a lawyer and he handles all my affairs. As a matter of fact, he comes out here twice a year."

"But you didn't want to marry him?" Harriet asked.

"He was already married when we met again," Toni said. "Unfortunately. Or maybe not unfortunately. It works out pretty well."

"You split up after the baby thing?"

"Not split up, exactly. When I got back home, he and his father were gone completely, and they wouldn't tell me where," Toni said.

"Has it upset you talking about all this?" Harriet said.

"Yup."

"And he — your lawyer…?"

"We never talk about it," Toni said. "He comes for a week, or longer if he can swing it. We play golf. Do a bit of fishing. Drive out to the Pacific Rim."

"That's where I'm planning on going when I leave here," Harriet said.

"By yourself?"

"I like driving," Harriet said. "It relaxes me. I guess the way you like playing golf and bridge."

"But I don't do them by myself," Toni said. "I have regular partners. That's the whole point."

"Oh," said Harriet, "regular partners."

XXIII

Everything that Toni had told her
matched perfectly with what Harriet already knew, for she had
fallen into Hope's role as inquisitor and pried every detail out of
Toni about her stay at their mother's apartment in Vancouver.
And Toni, visibly impatient to be rid of Harriet, had gone over
the story one more time before they parted. Finally, promising
to keep in touch (though they knew they wouldn't), they'd gone
their separate ways. And now Harriet, sitting in the window of
a hotel dining room overlooking the water, realized that at last
she understood everything she needed to know about her birth.

At first, Roger had told Nina not to worry, he'd take care of
everything. And he had so much power over so many people
that she hadn't doubted for a minute that he could do anything
he wanted to. He'd driven her across to the island on the ferry,
and he'd had two or three meetings with pulp mill executives
the way he always did. Then he'd taken her to the house by the
sea. It was November, and the place had been closed for the
winter. It was a cold spot on a promontory of land, bleak in the

winter, and so they never used it between November and February. In the big house, the furniture was covered with sheets, but he'd had someone light a fire in the gardener's cottage. The bed had been made up and the cottage was ready for use, the refrigerator and the kitchen cupboards well stocked.

That was where he left her to spend the next seven months. He'd get over when he could, he said, and there was a woman she could call on for help if she needed anything. But she didn't need anything, because there was a car she could use, and she could drive to the nearest village for her groceries. She had a radio and books. She read and walked a lot, and she was happy, not thinking much about what would happen later, trusting him to take care of it.

She was six months along when he told her on one of his flying visits that he had arranged a good home for it. She was so shocked, it was a wonder she didn't have the baby right then and there. What the hell had she thought would happen? he asked. Good question. What *had* she thought when he said not to worry? She thought he'd set her up in a little house or an apartment in Vancouver, and they'd live there, she and her little girl. (She was sure from the start that it would be a girl.) If she'd thought about anything in detail, it was who would look after the baby when she went back to work. And she did want to go back to work, because she didn't like the idea of him having another secretary. She wasn't that sure of his affections.

At first she'd cried and kicked up a fuss, but he set everything out reasonably. How could she take care of it? What kind of a life would it have? It wasn't so much that he convinced her as that he finally lost his patience and got mad, and she grew scared and realized she didn't have any choice. Then, after putting his foot down, he softened the blow. Once it was all over they'd go away somewhere for a wonderful holiday. Paris. How would she like Paris? He had some business he could do there.

After that, it wasn't much fun any more. It was all changed — the future, what she felt about him, everything. But he came over more often, and he was loving and kind. So she became reconciled until the next complication arose. That really threw him, and after he left he didn't even call for a while. He was out of the country on business. As soon as he got back, he came over again. This time he didn't say he'd take care of everything. He said it was one hell of a mess, and asked if there was any way she could take care of it herself. He was at his wit's end with business deals going awry, and now this, and he didn't even know now if he could get away for a vacation.

He asked if there were twins in her family, and she started to feel as if the whole thing was her own fault. She could think of only one solution, and she took it. Her sister had one kid and wanted more, but she wasn't able to have another. She'd had a breech birth and got all torn up when a country doctor with a drinking problem delivered the first one himself, instead of getting her to a hospital. If she wanted another one, there'd have to be a complicated operation that would cost a lot of money, without any guarantee of success. Nina didn't get on with her sister, but she braced herself, called up, confided in her, and asked if she'd like to adopt the kid. It would be all in the family, and from the same gene bank. Not one of these adoptions where you didn't know what you were getting.

It wasn't altogether straightforward because her sister imposed strict conditions. The kid was never to know where she came from. Nina could see her only as an aunt. There was to be no paperwork, no official adoption, nothing written down that anyone could ever trace. The only people who knew about it were Roger and Nina's brother-in-law. If the kid ever found out who her real mother was, Nina would never see her again, so she'd better be darn careful. Roger was so relieved by this arrangement that he started talking again about the wonderful holiday in France they'd have when it was all over.

It's strange to think of your own birth causing so much confusion and pain. But the part of the whole history that Harriet found the most unnerving was that she and Toni had been dispatched to their separate owners like a pair of puppies in need of a good home. And the choice of who went where was completely arbitrary. How had they decided? Had they given it any thought at all? She, Harriet, might so easily have been sent to Mazo and Caroline. Toni might have ended up on the farm. But Toni wasn't the least bit interested in what might have been.

Anyway, "the mess," as Roger tended to call it, had all blown over. He and Nina came back from Paris and carried on as if nothing had happened, just as he'd said they would. She'd found a home for one of the babies, and he'd taken care of the other. There was only one thing that didn't seem fair. He was forever asking about her niece, while at the same time he refused to tell her anything about what had happened to the other one. He said anonymity had been a condition of the adoption, as it was of most adoptions. And that was the end of it.

And then one day, quite by accident, she found out.

She was a member of his family by then. His wife and his sons all trusted and depended on her. If anyone needed an airline ticket or a reservation or travel plans, it was, "Ask Nina, she'll see to it." And she always did. She didn't feel put upon because they were always so grateful, and they expressed their gratitude very tangibly. They brought her wonderful presents when they came back. Her apartment was full of these gifts.

On the day she found out, she'd been invited to Sunday dinner because the boys had just got back from a trip to Europe, for which she'd made all the arrangements. They brought her back a lovely set of pearl earrings and a necklace from Majorca. Already they were being conditioned as young executives, as men who buy expensive jewelry for the women who grant them favours. They made her try them on then and there.

"We had a big argument about whether you'd prefer black pearls or white," they said. She laughed delightedly, flattered to think of them having an argument in some store on the island of Majorca about what kind of pearls she would prefer. Everyone agreed the white ones were preferable, and she looked marvellous in them.

After that, the conversation turned to the cousin who was a writer. The boys had visited her in England and finally met the daughter. Nina had known all along that Roger's wife had no time for Mazo and Caroline, suspecting that something funny was going on behind their façade of adopting each other as sisters. They were rarely discussed around the family dinner table, and when they visited the west coast Roger made an excuse for his wife's absence and saw them alone. Nina hadn't even known they had a daughter.

"How old is this Antoinette?" she asked.

"She's twelve," one of them said.

"Why, that's the same age as my niece," Nina said. Then she looked across the table at Roger. He reached out to fill up his wine glass, and she didn't need to ask any more. He had the tight look that he got around his mouth when he was angry. This time he wasn't the only one who was mad.

"I thought you said it would be an ordinary home, with people who could provide her with a normal life, which she wouldn't have if she stayed with me! What's normal about their life?"

By this time they were like a married couple whose spats follow a predictable pattern. First he frightened her with his anger. Then he tried to appease her with a bribe. The bribe this time was to give her two weeks off, tell her to invite Harriet out, and let them have the big house all to themselves for a holiday.

She hadn't counted on how upsetting it would be to be back at that place again.

And it wasn't only the memories that upset her. It was while she was there that she realized something else. It was the beginning of the end between them. He wouldn't marry her now for anything, even if he was free. He'd look out for her, but she'd be like a wife, without any of the advantages — just someone he had an obligation to that he couldn't shed. For companionship, he'd be on the lookout for someone else, one of the younger women, perhaps, who dimpled up to him around the office. And soon his boys would marry, and he'd have all the daughters and granddaughters he wanted. Gradually he'd forget he had any obligation towards her. He wouldn't even be concerned about his wife finding out about his fling with her. It would be all water under the bridge by then. It would be written off merely as a youthful indiscretion.

All this was going through Nina's mind while she was supposed to be enjoying herself, having a holiday at his beach house, with the daughter she could see for only two weeks, and who didn't even know who her real mother was.

Harriet could have burst into tears right there, sitting in the dining room window and looking out over the same stretch of water, thinking about it all these years later.

"Are you OK?" a voice said. It was the young waiter who'd been filling up her glass, and whom she noticed just then for the first time. Both his voice and his face were familiar, though she couldn't immediately place him.

"At the country club this morning," he prompted her. "I work both places, getting together enough to go back to school." It may or may not have been true, but it was a good ploy for getting tips.

"Should I help you up to your room?" he asked, sounding a little too familiar. And then by way of explanation, he said, "I sometimes help your sister home when she's…"

"Drunk?" Harriet said.

"Had one too many," he said, with a bartender's tact. "Who doesn't once in a while? You can't walk out with that carafe, anyway. It's against the rules. I'll have to bring it up."

The view from her room was the same as from the dining room. After he left, Harriet sat in the window and dialled Hope's number.

"Have you been drinking?" Hope said, but not censoriously. "Did it go off alright, the meeting?"

"Yes," Harriet said. "I've been reassessing that whole business with my mother and my father. I've finally figured out exactly what happened."

"When are you coming back so we can get on with planning the one-woman show?" Hope said after she'd heard the whole story. "This business with your aunt and Mazo and the rest of them — it's all over now, Harriet."

Hope's words fell on Harriet's ears like an echo from an earlier time. They *were* an echo.

It was the final night of the play. It happened to be a weekday, and by then Ted was back in the midst of his family. Bitha, with her tireless devotion, had rallied the class again, and there was a full house. During the first scene, to her amazement, Harriet spotted Blanche, Archie, and Lilian in her wheelchair, all sitting in the front row. In the row behind, she saw the shaven head of Toby, and close by she saw two other familiar faces that she couldn't immediately place.

Archie's restlessness increased during the play, and by the end of the second act he'd disappeared. His guardians remained in the theatre, either too engrossed in the play to notice his absence or confident that he would gravitate to the bar and not have time to do irreparable damage before they retrieved him and took him home.

Apart from the fact that the portrait of Mazo was unaccountably missing from its place when the first act began, the last performance was marked for Harriet by one other significant event. When it came to the part about the adoption of Mazo's daughter, followed by the digression that Brandi had come to expect, Harriet reverted to Hope's original script. She followed it faithfully, word for word, as if whatever had caused the detour had finally been exorcised.

At the end, the audience applauded with great enthusiasm, some of the regular theatre-goers struggling to their feet to join the students who had bounced up to give the players a standing ovation. It was when she and Brandi were brought out for the third time by the applause that Harriet remembered where she'd seen the familiar couple. They were the surly bride and groom whose wedding she'd watched in the park that Saturday in August. Harriet smiled directly at them, and they both smiled back at her. She took it as a good sign that they seemed to be clinging together very closely.

She was thinking about them and still smiling when she ran off stage for the last time. She almost bumped into Hope, who spread out her arms and hugged her.

"It's all over now, Harriet," Hope said.

For you, but not for me, Harriet thought.

But this time Hope was right. It *was* over for her too.

XXIV

Harriet woke up in an unfamiliar room, with the red sticks of a digital clock radio on the bedside table reconfiguring themselves with alarming speed. She was hung over, naturally, having followed the carafe of wine with some little bottles of Scotch from the well-stocked fridge; she struggled to consciousness out of a swirl of disquieting dreams. Still, a hint of bright sunshine leaked through a gap in the curtains.

She drew them apart to reveal a view of spectacular beauty — an expanse of still water against a backdrop of mountains, the sun rising in a sky the colour of salmon flesh, sea birds crying, early fishing boats moving out. She made coffee, carefully following the instructions on the machine, while listening to a cello concerto by Elgar on the radio.

The familiar chords announcing the CBC news sounded just as she poured out her first cup of coffee. She moved to switch off the radio, but not before the words "This is an extended election edition" jolted her completely awake.

"I have no intention of dying," Lilian had told her at their first meeting, "before the next election."

Lilian would be alone in her rooms, struggling to dress and get from her bedroom into the sitting room to make her morning tea. She could have slipped and fallen down, be lying unconscious on the floor, and it would be hours before Mrs. Pike arrived.

But when Harriet dialled Lilian's number, the phone was picked up promptly. As clearly as if Harriet was standing in the doorway looking at her, she could see Lilian sitting in her chintz-covered armchair by the fireplace in Fortescue Street, the bedroom door slightly open, and Archie's painting in its place over the bed.

"Oh, it's you, Harriet," she said. "How am I? Exasperated is how I am. Very exasperated and very disillusioned. Perhaps more disillusioned than exasperated. Did you hear the election results? Sometimes one wonders if people have any sense at all, and if they even deserve good government. And another four years to sit out with these present crooks running things."

Lilian grumbled on for quite a while, and Harriet listened patiently, sipping her coffee, reassured by the thought of Lilian sitting out the next four years. Finally Lilian's irritation at the election results ran its course, and her mind turned to other matters.

"I'm so glad you phoned, Harriet, because there are several messages for you."

Bitha had called to ask when she'd be back. Ted had left a message to say he'd had to fly to Ottawa on short notice and asking her to call him collect at his hotel there in the evening. Lilian wasn't sure which evening that was. A gentleman from Vancouver had been trying to get hold of her on what he said was a matter of great urgency and had been quite rude. Not a gentleman at all, really. Lilian had finally told him it was no use calling her again, because she hadn't the faintest idea of Harriet's whereabouts. He had left his name and number.

"I hope I didn't give offence," Lilian said, "but he was really getting to be a nuisance."

"Where the hell have you been, Harriet, and where in god's name are you at?" he said when Harriet reached him. "I've been trying to find you for days. I wish you'd stop doing these goddamn disappearing acts. There's hell to pay when somebody wants you, and the old bitch at your rooming house said she didn't think you'd be coming back. Anyway, here you are. You'd better sit down, this is a plum — that's if they haven't got someone else by this time."

Harriet sat down, thinking of her disappearing acts. Someone else had said the same thing. She watched the sun rise higher and she saw the salmon-coloured sky change to bright blue, almost as if it were a midsummer day. It seemed to her, as she looked at it, that her whole life up to this point had been a disappearing act. She listened as he ranted on about her good luck and his superhuman efforts on her behalf and his refusal to give up on her, in spite of her dicey reputation and other liabilities, too numerous to mention.

And, tuning in and tuning out, murmuring occasional thanks, confirming that she was still with him, but too bowled over by her good fortune and his colossal achievement to say much except "thank you," and that yes, she was ready to take the part, and yes, she could get to the airport as soon as possible, and yes, she could be ready for rehearsals almost at once. He wouldn't need to courier a copy of the script to her this time. She didn't need it immediately. After all, it was a part she was familiar with, because it hadn't been so long since she'd played it before. "Yes," she said, "yes, I will, yes…"

Just a short time ago, the prospect of playing Bernhardt again would have terrified her, but now she felt no fear — of the role or of her capacity for it or of what would happen when the run ended and left her cut adrift once more.

When she called for the second time, Lilian answered as promptly as before and continued the conversation as if there had been no interruption.

"My father used to say that democracy doesn't ensure good government, it ensures only that you don't have a dictatorship. But there's no point having a democracy unless you have an educated public that is willing to read and able to reason. You might just as well have a dictator, because there's the same danger of oppression and tyranny, and ultimately, yes, fascism. Look what happens in the United States. Elections have turned into popularity contests, as if they were choosing the captain of a cheerleading squad in junior high school. They pick the most photogenic and charismatic candidate, and it hardly matters that, if he ever had a brain, it softened into imbecility long ago. I wish you could do a play about this, and I've said as much to Hope and offered to give her some ideas. But Hope doesn't always see the connections between things. I liked her play very much, Harriet, but I would like to see you both do something that's, you know, more socially engaged."

When she finally ran out of steam, Harriet managed to break the news that she'd been offered a part in a big theatre production down east. She had to take it up immediately and wouldn't have time to come back to Fortescue Street. It was a severe blow to her pride that Lilian accepted the news with equanimity and was not the least bit upset by it.

"That's very good for you, Harriet. I thought all along that you shouldn't, you know, bury yourself in this small place, happy as we were to have you among us for a time. It's as good a place as any, in its way, but it *is* a small town. The trouble is that if you stay here too long, you lose your perspective. You start thinking of it as the centre of the universe, and then you become ridiculous. And don't worry about your possessions. You travel light, and it will be an easy matter to…"

Harriet strained to learn the fate of her possessions, but Lilian's explanation was lost in the background noise. At first Harriet had thought there was a bad connection on the line, but then she realized that she was hearing the monotonous beat of a percussion instrument. It was getting gradually louder.

"Lilian," she said, "what's that noise?"

"It's my nephew," Lilian said. "He has a good sense of rhythm, but he needs to learn more varied rhythmic patterns. His playing leaves much to be desired at the moment, but it will improve with time. He has been using the attic temporarily, but now that you no longer need it.…"

Harriet didn't know whether to be pleased or alarmed on Toby's account.

"What about Blanche?" she said.

"Blanche is here too," Lilian said. "She's hoping to open a small restaurant, and she's very busy with plans for it just now. We've been looking through my files for reviews of theatrical productions. I believe she intends to frame them in some way and hang them on the wall."

"But what about Archie? How will he manage without her?" Harriet said.

"Oh, he'll be absolutely furious. There'll be a huge blow-up, and he'll accuse me of ruining his life as usual. But Blanche will be much better off with me. I'll keep the piano tuned, and that might induce her to play again, if only for her own pleasure. Or

mine. And if she doesn't play, well, that's not very important. She'll have a home, and she'll be good company for me. And there's no need to worry about Archie. There are hordes of women only too eager to look after him. His brand of helplessness always attracts female protectors. The world is very kind to men like Archie, Harriet."

There was a pause during which the drum beat got louder and then faded.

"There's another thing I have to tell you, Harriet, since I won't be seeing you again. I have a confession. It was I who removed your whisky before the play. I know I shouldn't have. It was an inexcusable intrusion, but it was done with the best of intentions. I was worried, you know."

"But how did you get up there?" Harriet said.

"I can summon up the strength when the occasion warrants it. There's a pill I take for such times. There are pills available these days for all purposes and eventualities. I have little stores of them hidden about the place, and I keep them in reserve to use at times of crisis. I watched the election results on the television sets up there. Let me give you a piece of advice, Harriet. It's unwise to let people know the full extent of your resources. They tend to take advantage. And keeping that knowledge in reserve gives you a modicum of power you wouldn't otherwise have."

When Harriet said she would miss Lilian very much, she was saddened that the sentiment wasn't returned. Lilian didn't even urge Harriet to phone or write or keep in touch.

"I expect we shall read about you in the papers," she said. "I shall clip and collect all your notices. You'll be an important part of my archival record. I've already got a file labelled 'HARRIET,' and I've put the reviews of Hope's play in it. And Hope says she has some very interesting material to contribute to it."

Hope, thought Harriet. She was tempted to put off speaking to Hope until she was settled in her new surroundings and well outside Hope's sphere of influence. But she braced herself to get it over with. Once it was done, she would be able to drive to the airport with a clear conscience, turn in the rented car, catch her flight to Toronto, and concentrate single-mindedly on Sarah Bernhardt.

"Well, that's good for you," Hope said when Harriet told her about the change of plans. She sounded strangely uninterested in Harriet's future. Like Lilian, Hope seemed to have other things on her mind, and her readiness to surrender their one-woman show was another blow to Harriet's pride. Harriet was reminded once again of how unimportant she was in other people's lives. She had to face the fact one more time that she would never come first in anyone else's affections.

"You know," Hope said, "I've been thinking a lot about Toby. That boy has enormous potential. He has great stage presence, and I believe he would make a fine actor if only we could get him some vocal training."

"In a play of your own?" Harriet said.

"Oh, no," Hope said, "Sandy was quite right. I'm not a dramatist. I don't have what it takes. I see that now."

"Sandy isn't right about everything," Harriet said. "It was a really original idea you had."

"It was original," Hope said, "but it didn't work."

Harriet was tempted to argue the point, but she said merely that she was sorry Hope felt their play had all been wasted effort.

"Not wasted effort, by any means," Hope said. "I didn't say that. I just said it didn't work. I see now that the whole play thing was crucial to the evolution of the biography. It's a complicated thing when you undertake someone's life. It's like assuming a role.

I see that very clearly now. The play was a step on the way to something else. It was not so much a digression as the laying down of
important groundwork. It was a parenthetical experience, but it
was crucial. That's probably a paradox."

It was true all the same, Harriet thought. The play had been
a digression for her, too, but at the same time, it had been crucial.

Once she was airborne, Harriet began the process of sub-
merging her life in Bernhardt's once again. She thought about
Sarah's love affair with the Prince de Ligne. He'd been one of her
first lovers, perhaps the very first, and he was the father of her only
child. She was twenty years old at the time, and the match was
impossible. His family threatened to disown him, and he was too
weak, or too young and immature, to face the life of an outcast.
Sarah told her grandchildren that his uncle had pleaded with her
to make the noble gesture of renunciation, and she had agreed to
do so. Maybe that version of events owed something to the second
act of *La Dame aux Camellias*. She'd played Marguerite Gauthier
over two hundred times, and it was possible she no longer distinguished between her own past and Marguerite's. On the other
hand, perhaps the overwhelming power for her performance came
from a long buried memory. It was impossible to separate the two
— Bernhardt's own life and the role in the play.

The final act of her personal drama had played itself out
when she was at the height of her fame. The prince, after many
years, came to see her and to meet his son. For one brief
moment — an hour? an afternoon? a whole day? — they were
a family, made up of father, mother, and their child. The prince
was so impressed by the young man that he offered him the gift
of his illustrious name. The offer was declined.

Later Maurice escorted his father to the Gare du Nord for
his return to Brussels. The prince approached a guard and told

him, "I am the Prince de Ligne." It brought no response, but then Maurice stepped forward and said, "I am the son of Sarah Bernhardt." The two were immediately treated with deference.

They'd flown beyond the cloud cover and the mountain ranges, and they were now over the prairies. When Harriet looked down, she could see the patchwork of fields, the scattered farms, and then a city with streets and buildings and parks and a lake.

"Would you like something from the bar?" the flight attendant asked. She had to lean over two other passengers to get Harriet's attention. When she finally did, Harriet turned away from the window. Seeing the city from above, so dwindled and vulnerable, its inhabitants going about their business without her, had given her a moment of panic, but it was brief, and it soon passed.

"A double Scotch," she said automatically. And then she changed her mind and asked for a glass of white wine. As she drank it, she was intoxicated by the thought that very soon she'd be playing Sarah Bernhardt again.